Midnight Movie Monographs

PLAN 9 FROM OUTER SPACE

Midnight Movie Monographs

PLAN 9 FROM OUTER SPACE

A Monograph on Bad Film

Katharine Coldiron

Electric Dreamhouse
Midnight Movie Monographs

Midnight Movie Monographs

PLAN 9 FROM OUTER SPACE

Series Editor
Neil Snowdon

Published in October 2021 by Electric Dreamhouse, an imprint of PS Publishing Ltd. by arrangement with the author.

First Edition

ISBN
978-1-786363-42-8

Design & Layout by Michael Smith
Printed and bound in England by T.J. Books

PS Publishing
Grosvenor House
1 New Road
Hornsea, HU18 1PG
England

editor@pspublishing.co.uk
www.pspublishing.co.uk

CONTENTS

ix . . . . Author's Note

3. . . . . I: Analysis

33. . . . . II: Exegesis

87. . . . . III: In Sum

97. . . . . Bibliography

98. . . . . Acknowledgements

Perhaps none of our films have, so far, been up for awards, but they are entertaining pictures.

—Edward D. Wood, Jr., *Hollywood Rat Race*

How much can you say? He tried, mostly failed, and died.

—Ted Newsom, *The Cinematic Misadventures of Ed Wood*

UNSPEAKABLE HORRORS FROM OUTER SPACE PARALYZE THE LIVING AND RESURRECT THE DEAD!
PLAN 9 FROM OUTER SPACE
with
BELA LUGOSI
VAMPIRA
LYLE TALBOT
A J. Edward Reynolds Production
Produced and Directed by
Edward D. Wood, Jr.
a DCA release

AUTHOR'S NOTE

THANKS FOR READING THIS.

The two sections of this monograph overlap. I wrote it so that you can choose to read just one or the other, rather than both, if you'd like. The central theses of this long essay exist in both places.

It was difficult to determine how to give names to the characters/actors in *Plan 9 from Outer Space* as I write about them. It would be foolish to call Tor Johnson by his character's name once he is undead, because his bulk and reputation are so clearly the point of his casting; similarly, Bela Lugosi is never given a proper character name. However, other actors are more obscure than these two, so I think of them with the characters' names rather than the actors'. The movie doesn't do a particularly adequate job introducing some of them, though. To save us both a headache, here's a *dramatis personae*:

Jeff Trent (Gregory Walcott) = the husband/pilot
Paula Trent (Mona McKinnon) = the wife
Col. Edwards (Tom Keene) = military guy "in charge of saucer field activity"
Inspector Clay (Tor Johnson) = huge bald dude who becomes ghoul
Eros (Dudley Manlove) = main alien, very smug
Tanna (Joanna Lee) = female alien, not a lot of lines
Ruler (John "Bunny" Breckinridge) = alien in charge; bulging, sleepy eyes

Lt. Harper (Duke Moore) = policeman in the trenchcoat
Larry (Carl Anthony) = low-voiced policeman
Kelton (Paul Marco) = bumbling policeman
Gen. Roberts (Lyle Talbot) = military guy who assigns Edwards to cemetery
Vampira (Maila Nurmi) = Vampira, wife of the old man, only seen as ghoul
Old Man (Bela Lugosi) = real Lugosi, starts alive and becomes ghoul
Dead Old Man (Tom Mason) = faux-Lugosi, ghoul with cape over face
Criswell (Criswell) = narrator, platinum blond guy who opens and closes movie

The film takes place in a handful of locations: a plane cockpit, the patio of a house, the inside of a spaceship. It's not hard to distinguish these, to refer to them and be understood. However, one major location, a cemetery, is multiple.

Cemetery (a), the location cemetery

Scenes with Bela Lugosi were evidently shot in a real cemetery in Sacramento (a).[1] Scenes with other characters meant to be at the cemetery were shot somewhere outdoors, not necessarily at a cemetery at all, and almost certainly not in Sacramento (b).[2] One still photograph, used repeatedly for process shots, is likely of a cemetery in Los Angeles, although my research has not uncovered which one (c). Finally, many scenes take place in a "cemetery" setting that's clearly in a studio, as the scenery is unconvincing and the lighting is artificial (d). I refer to (a) and (b) as "the location cemetery," (c) as "the photo cemetery" or similar, and (d) as "the studio cemetery."

Cemetery (c), the photo cemetery

It's useful to distinguish these locales when the film cuts back and forth between them. However, the filmmaker clearly intends for them all to be one single location. Since the gap between intention and execution is

[1] According to Ed Wood in *Nightmare of Ecstasy*. I don't understand how this is possible, as it means he took Lugosi, then quite frail, from Los Angeles all the way to Sacramento, in the cars and on the roads of 1955-6, just to film a few scenes. That seems highly unlikely. I don't think I'm misinterpreting his storytelling in the book, but his wording isn't perfectly clear.

[2] Possibly in Sylmar, per *The Cinematic Misadventures of Ed Wood*.

part of what I'm studying here, we need to understand both, particularly with regard to the cemetery. Thus, each of the locations has a separate nickname, even though they're all meant, per the filmmaker, to be the same place.

Cemetery (d), the studio cemetery

If this seems confusing, well, we're on the right track.

Plan 9 from Outer Space is in the public domain. The quotes from the screenplay are a mix of my own transcription, a transcribed version found on the internet,[3] and the authorized original screenplay edited by Tom Mason and published in 1990 by Malibu Graphics. (A full bibliography is available at the end of this volume.) I mixed these sources in order to make sense of inconsistencies. For example, the neologism "Solaronite" is pronounced differently than it appears in the published script, so I went with the script. Meanwhile, Col. Edwards is named Col. Rance in the script, so I went with the finished film.

As I reviewed the script against the close readings I did on certain scenes, I found that some of the film's smaller and more absurd contradictions did not exist in Wood's words. Some of the word choices that appear in the

[3] From horrorlair.com.

film were evidently mistakes by the actors, late scene changes, or cuts in the editing room, potentially due to unusable film. It's not my intention to unfairly ridicule Edward D. Wood, Jr. or his work by ignoring any actual logic in his screenplay and instead highlighting the illogic that wound up on the screen. I want to give him credit where it's due. Whenever I analyze a flaw in the film that is not a flaw in the screenplay, I'll footnote it with the written lines. If I don't remark on the differences, either the screenplay matches the film or the difference is irrelevant. I will note this again later, but the point to know now is that I do not wish to be cruel to Wood when he doesn't deserve it.

That said, if an actor makes a mistake that causes a scene to stop making sense, you *reshoot the scene* with the correct line. Wood was famously uninterested in retakes, either for mistakes or for coverage, and so, if his finished scenes fail to make sense, it's still his fault.

The film was shot in 1956 and released in limited runs for a couple of years, until the official run began in 1959. As such, I refer to multiple years in what follows, depending on whether I'm talking about filming or release. It's not sloppy editing. Also, the film was shot in black and white, but a colorized version appeared around 2006.

All emphasis in quoted dialogue is mine.

A monograph is a weird undertaking. I wrote this one about *Plan 9* because I knew I wanted one essay to gather up all my best thoughts about bad movies. Please indulge me if I stray too far off the point.

PLAN 9
FROM
OUTER
SPACE
with
BELA LUGOSI
VAMPIRA
LYLE TALBOT
A J. Edward Reynolds Production
Produced and Directed by
Edward D. Wood, Jr.
a DCA release
4
58-294

I: ANALYSIS

(1) EXTRAORDINARY

AS WITH MANY FILMS THAT HAVE CHANGED MY LIFE, SUCCORED my days, kept me warm when I felt the cold world, I have no memory of the first time I saw *Plan 9 from Outer Space*. One day it was not in my life, and the next day, immutably, it was. I doubt I was fully a child when I saw the movie, and I know it doesn't belong to a situation where I saw it on TV one afternoon in adolescence and let the memory sleep until I needed to waken it. The watching was certainly deliberate, but information on how it took place is not available.

In my late teens, my father started collecting DVDs of all possible quality—everything from *La Dolce Vita* to *They Saved Hitler's Brain*.[4] Certainly *Plan 9* was among them. I doubt that was the first time I'd heard of it, though. Just the most likely occasion for me to run into it.

A memory I can't disconnect from *Plan 9* is advertisements for a record store in Charlottesville, Virginia. I lived there between ages 11 and 13, late 1992 to early 1995, and a very cool record store named Plan 9 operated there. (A small blessing: it still operates as of this writing.) The store used clips from the movie in its TV ads, particularly a duplicated audio bite of Dudley Manlove saying "Plan 9, Plan 9," from the scene where Eros explains his progress to his fey, uninterested boss. From this distance I love

[4] Actually an interesting film. It was mostly shot in the early 1960s and then finished by a group of 1970s film students, and you can really tell which scenes were shot when because of the clothes. The Hitler sequences involve the Fuhrer's head in a bottle, just like on *Futurama*, and he's as much of a monster to the unlucky characters in the film as any giant bug. The head dies in a fire at the end.

that someone named their record store after this movie, and that they elected to use the movie in their ads. But I got it backwards because of my age: I knew about the store before the movie.

Anyway, I don't remember the first time I saw *Plan 9 from Outer Space*, and thus I don't remember my first impressions. Never at any time did I believe I was sitting down to watch a good movie, which means I never gave it a chance to be good, not until I'd come to know it better. I knew the film's reputation going in; I knew I was watching it because it was not good.

Why would anyone do this? It's perverse. At first glance, it doesn't make sense—setting yourself up for a negative experience. At the time, in all likelihood, I was doing it to laugh, to have fun at *Plan 9*'s expense. I learned the practice from my father, who learned it from I know not where. *Mystery Science Theater 3000*, possibly, although he was well into adulthood when he found that show. Based on how gleefully he embraced bad movies, I can't believe he didn't have an existing attraction to them when *MST3K* came around.

It's a big question, *why watch bad movies*, and I'm tempted to set it aside for later and get going on *Plan 9*. But, in a way, it's the entire question of this project. If *Plan 9* has any worth at all, it's not because it's any good. It's because it's bad. That badness must have some worthwhile quality, or this project has an empty purpose. The problem could swing philosophical, where I try to define what "good" and "bad" are and what value exists in each. But that seems far afield, when my purpose here is limited to the value, specifically, of *Plan 9 from Outer Space*, of what the film has to show us both literally and figuratively.

Some personalities attract to bad movies because they are bullies and like to laugh at the expense of others. Some enjoy watching what happens when things go wrong. But some—and I've grown into this; I doubt I considered it when I first saw *Plan 9*—want to compare a film going sideways to a film going straight. *Plan 9* is terrible in a rainbow of ways, from conception to completion, from technical to tactical. In picking apart all these flaws and mistakes, I can see and understand why good films work. I'm convinced, in fact, that it's easier to understand good film by examining bad film than by examining good film.

It strikes me, trying to remember how *Plan 9* entered my life, that I watched all those bad movies my dad bought on DVD at around the same time I awakened to film as an art form. I didn't realize how thoroughly my brain was built to analyze film until mid-college, but by then I'd seen dozens of classics, written lengthy emails to friends and mentors about Paul Thomas Anderson and Quentin Tarantino, started building a DVD collection of my own. And all the time I was absorbing Hitchcock and Lynch and the Coens and Bergman and Deren and Buñuel and Dreyer and Keaton, I was watching schlock from the 50s, slashers from the 80s, no-budget garbage from multiple decades.

It all happened at the same time: dizzying heights of fine film, hilarious lows of bad movies. Eventually they became connected in my mind. Eventually I saw that one is not possible without the other, and that a full education in film must include both, possibly in equal abundance.

Such an education might well begin with *Plan 9 from Outer Space*. There exists a canon of bad movies, just as there is of good, and *Plan 9* is as indispensable on one list as *Citizen Kane* is on the other. It commits every mistake, and fails in every particular.[5] We go to the movies to see something extraordinary, no matter what or when or wherefore. And *Plan 9* most assuredly is extraordinary.

(2) CONTEXT

I'm not sure whether I'm writing this with the assumption that you have or haven't seen *Plan 9 from Outer Space*. Do people read monographs about objects they aren't already familiar with? To learn about them prior to experiencing them? That's valid, but it feels odd. No one writes a monograph without obsession, and obsession is repellent without a notion of its object.

As a critic I always write somewhere in the middle of the assumption that you have or haven't been here before. I summarize the book or movie as competently and briefly as possible, providing what I hope is a reasonable picture to those who don't know the work without boring the

[5] With minor exceptions. We'll get there.

folks who do. That's a bit of an art form in itself. The summary must not leave out anything important, nor stuff in too much detail, and it must be lively. If the object under examination is complicated, or bad, or character-driven, the challenge multiplies. I've occasionally cheated by saying my space is too limited to go into a full plot summary, or by pretending I'm writing a trailer script and speaking in taglines. *Will he get the girl? Will she overcome her past? Who's out to get them? It's a race against time to uncover the real truth about this heartfelt confession.* I hope my reader rolls her eyes as she understands that I'm trying to make her roll her eyes.

All that considered, here's a summary of *Plan 9 from Outer Space*. Aliens, unhappy with Earth's irresponsibility with regard to weaponry, hatch a plot to get through to us: reanimate the corpses of the recently deceased,[6] who will then terrify and/or kill citizens, which will cause the leaders of Earth to do what the aliens say. As 1950s movies go, this plot is hardly the stupidest or least likely ever dreamed up. What makes it fall apart like tissues in water is the relationship of the plot to actual scenes appearing in the movie. The plot outlined in this summary isn't really part of the movie until 20 minutes in. Understanding the plot requires understanding that the majority of the movie doesn't necessarily advance the plot much.

The different sequences of *Plan 9* perform like a network of ideas, not all of which connect to each other. These ideas don't proceed logically, one after the other, and do not receive parallel screen time to unfold. I tried to chart the connections between major sequences or plotlines in the film. These charts were so tangled they didn't make sense. That is: all the action in the film attaches to one of nine elements,[7] but some of the elements are only connected to one or two others, while others act more centrally but still don't connect to all nine. All the ideas are in the same movie, but they don't all cross paths onscreen. Here's a list of the major sequences or plotlines, in order of how much they connect to each other:

[6] The word "zombie" is never used. The history of zombies in film is available elsewhere, but in short, "zombie" was not so common a word in the genre film of the late 1950s as it would be a decade later, after *Night of the Living Dead*. I have used the words "undead" or "ghouls" throughout this text; the film mostly uses "the dead," which is unnecessarily vague, and later on uses "ghouls."

[7] Pure coincidence that there are nine plot elements in *Plan 9 from Outer Space*.

1. Jeff and Paula Trent
2. Criswell
3. Flying Saucers
4. Aliens and Plan 9
5. Cemetery Activity
6. Colonel Edwards
7. Bela Lugosi Sequence
8. Policemen
9. Piloting

"Piloting" only connects to two other elements in the film (the Trents and the flying saucers), and not to the policemen, the cemetery activity, or the sequence early in the film with Bela Lugosi. Meanwhile, the Trents connect to *six* other aspects of the plot (the policemen, the cemetery activity, Col. Edwards, the flying saucers, the Lugosi sequence, and piloting). But Paula and Jeff Trent are not the primary plot of *Plan 9*. The aliens and the plan are, and they only connect directly to five other elements (the Hollywood montage, the cemetery activity, the Lugosi sequence, the Trents, and Col. Edwards).

The film comes off as a disaster on a macro level for the same reason I couldn't visually chart the plot: lack of structure, balance, or connection between sequences. While logical enough when summarized, the plot *seems* not to make any sense. It might have if it was presented in the right way, with the aliens and their plan front and center. Placing them there would mean giving the aliens scenes early and often, connecting the aliens to the ghouls clearly, cutting out some of the pointless scenes with the policemen and with Lugosi, and showing the threads coming together in such a way that the audience can make sense of it slightly before it happens.

However, in the film, some of the sequences don't connect to each other at all, while others connect in illogical ways. Criswell, for instance, opens and closes the film with awkward, vaguely doomsaying speeches, and provides voiceover to (attempt to) tie various scenes together. But he's a strange, clumsy narrator, the stock footage he narrates serves as filler, and his voiceover comes and goes so irregularly that it just forms one more untethered element, a piece of a puzzle that never becomes complete. I can see what the film was trying to do with Criswell's narration, but it fails. Badly.

Already I'm looking behind the camera for an explanation of why *Plan 9* is so bad, instead of making sense of it as a finished product. That's my special gift (or curse): I am ever Toto, pulling back the curtain on the flawed and mortal Wizard of Oz. I get that Bela Lugosi doesn't really exist as part of the same film the other actors are in because the poor man died, and the film was written around existing footage of him.[8] Offscreen context helps a flaw like this to make sense (even if it does not erase the flaw), instead of just existing on the screen for me to pillory. I get that the acting is mostly bad because Wood could not afford decent actors. I get that takes are bad because Wood had to shoot the film on an unimaginably short timeline and wouldn't or couldn't reshoot bad takes. I can perceive the motivations of this film's mistakes even as I note them, laugh at them, refuse to overlook them.

That's what it means to appreciate bad film. Comprehending the cost of good film and the machinery of Hollywood, learning as much context as possible, and picking apart the reasons bad films fall short by understanding *what* they were trying to do, *why* they did what they did instead, and *how* those choices led to failure. *Plan 9*'s ambitions aren't especially distinguished—it played as part of a double feature[9] with a couple of film noirs and *Devil Girl from Mars*—but the calculated compromises of even those minor ambitions help to elucidate the project's failures.

For example: how running time necessitates stock footage.[10] When Wood was making films, any film's running time had to hit a certain number to be acceptable to distributors and theaters. Using stock footage

---

[8] In *Nightmare of Ecstasy*, Paul Marco says Wood wrote the screenplay around some of the cast members Marco introduced him to. However, it seems much more likely, based on material in the published screenplay and accounts about the productions Wood was trying to mount in 1956, that the screenplay was written primarily to use the footage Wood had shot with Lugosi.

[9] http://movieline.com/2009/09/08/plan-9-from-outer-space-the-original-bad-movie-we-love-turns-50/

[10] Stock footage is film that can be reused without attendant rights issues. Generally it's footage of crowds, landmarks, or otherwise generic material. A modern example is shots of unidentifiable people (heads cut off or faces indistinct) that appear on the news when the reporters are talking in voiceover about a perennial health issue like smoking or obesity.

is much less expensive than shooting new footage, which involves paying actors, renting a studio, using props, and buying film. Using what amounts to public domain material is a cheap way to pad out a movie. Thus, one strategy to increase the running time for any given B movie, so as to make it acceptable to distributors, is incorporating stock footage. Knowing that chain of circumstance helps us understand why there is stock footage in *Plan 9*, and thus makes our ability to empathize with its failures that much stronger.

Why should we empathize with its failures at all? Why not dismiss bad film and go on about our jobs in cinema (creative, critical, scholarly) without seeing and studying the worst of it? If I fail to convince you across this monograph that bad film is profoundly instructive about the art and craft of cinema, here's another reason: all art exists on a spectrum, and it's difficult to appreciate the furthest end of the good side if you lack full familiarity with the furthest end of the bad side. A good, musical sentence may be pleasing, but if all you ever read and hear are good, musical sentences, how can you grasp the work and talent that go into them? How will you ever gain perspective about which end of the spectrum the art you absorb lives in? How will you ever understand how much further to the other side that spectrum goes? Surrounding oneself only with good art is how critics become isolated from the range of creative work that exists, how they become ever more specialized, how they find themselves in tiny, rarefied biospheres of good art of only a particular variety.

I am hardly the first to say this, but it bears repeating: growing as an artist or critic can only occur through an omnivorous diet for art. As an example from my own diet, I've read barely any horror outside of Stephen King, so I have no sense of whether he's one of the best writers in the genre or one of the worst. I can guess, based on his reputation, but I can't trust that guess any further than I can trust the whims of the marketplace.

Reading and watching in multiple genres is essential, but that's about breadth of diet, and true omnivores attain depth, as well. Without bad poetry, we cannot recognize good poetry. As long as absorbing bad art doesn't lead to complacency,[11] that absorption can only increase our

[11] Avoid the tempting shortcut of "at least I'm a better writer than William McGonagall" if you ever want to improve.

capacity to understand what we create. And although analyzing good art leads us to a strong understanding of why it works as it does—indeed, it's the entire model of arts education—analyzing bad art is faster, and can even be more fun.

(3) AUTEUR

At some point we must talk about the filmmaker, Edward D. Wood, Jr., whose reputation may precede him into these pages. Johnny Depp memorably portrayed him in Tim Burton's *Ed Wood* (1994), which concludes with the first screening of *Plan 9*. It's a very good and interesting film, one that makes an optimistic but misguided hero out of Wood. Yet I think it would be a mistake to assume that film does more than sketch the real human being Edward D. Wood, Jr. was. It hardly accounts for his many depressing years drinking through scummy films like *Necromania* and *Drop-Out Wife*.

It also doesn't explain the peculiar condition shared by Wood, Tommy Wiseau, Claudio Fragasso, James Nguyen, and many others: the conviction that the movies they make have genuine quality. It's a unique delusion, this incapacity to see what divides their films from, say, Alfred Hitchcock's or Dario Argento's. And it's not as if these filmmakers think they're just doing something different, but valid; they genuinely do not understand why the wider public rewards other directors with Oscars and boffo box office and not them. Wiseau submitted *The Room* to the Academy Awards in all seriousness. In *Best Worst Movie*, Fragasso repeatedly defends *Troll 2* as if it is a perfectly fine and normal horror movie instead of the surreal trainwreck it truly is. And, well, here's James Nguyen on the special effects in *Birdemic*:

> *From a distance, I think those eagles and vultures look pretty shocking and terrifying. And they come a little closer, maybe more shocking and terrifying. And when you get close up to them, they look different. It's something new, something you haven't seen before. Maybe it's art.*[12]

---

[12] https://bloody-disgusting.com/interviews/23593/special-interview-birdemic-shock-and-terror-director-

I can't make sense of this condition. James Nguyen and I both watch *The Birds*, and we both watch *Birdemic: Shock and Terror*, and yet what he sees in each film and what I see in each film are radically different conceptions of the same material. How he can sense that the one is good, and fail to sense that the other is bad, I do not understand. Interpretation of a film, and a judgment of its quality by degrees—these are subjective critical comparisons. But I see that Nguyen's framing is lousy, his timing is inhumanly poor, his visual style is amateurish at best and nonexistent at worst, and his actor guidance is meaningless. And I see that Hitchcock is a master of all these qualities. Nguyen does not see any of this. He sees no distinction. In both films he sees good movies.

It's like that old philosophical problem of never *really* knowing that I'm seeing the same color as you are when we both call something blue, because maybe I've just learned to call blue what you call red. Are we seeing different movies, somehow? Are our two brains processing them differently?

Wood's angle on this condition has to do with "good enough," if Burton's portrait of him is to be believed. Or possibly "the audience won't notice." But how can the audience not notice? How can this work be good enough? In some of the shots of Colonel Edwards alone in a white abyss with a pair of binoculars, you can see the material of the dropcloth behind him slightly bunch along the bottom third of the screen, an indication that he isn't standing in front of, uh, the sky. Maybe drive-in audiences wouldn't notice that. But a gravestone that waggles like cardboard when an ambulance attendant kicks it? Blatant cuts between day and night shots within mere moments of story time? A momentum-draining cut trying to hide the fact that Tor Johnson couldn't struggle out of a grave on his own? Come on. The audience is not blind. If they don't notice these things, they are not watching this inherently visual medium.

And how can Wood, with his metatextual knowledge of how films are made, forgive such obvious flaws? Or is that metatextual knowledge the reason he believes the audience doesn't see them? Because he has fallen in love with the way a rectangular frame transforms a set into a universe, does he believe he can fool an audience into accepting *anything* inside that frame?

---

james-nguyen/. Not one word of this quote is objectively true.

PLAN 9 FROM OUTER SPACE

Viewers with no experience in bad film sometimes think that makers of bad movies must dislike, or disrespect, the art form. How could they, why would they, besmirch it so if they loved it? Don't they see the mockery they make of cinema? But that isn't how it works. Edward D. Wood, Jr. *loved* movies. He loved the wonder of them, the out-of-body of them, the way a good movie makes itself a wide-open possibility space and invites you inside. These are qualities *Plan 9 from Outer Space* attempts, almost bravely, and totally fails to convey. It's a bad movie because, at bottom, *it is unconvincing as a movie*.

Where *Plan 9* succeeds valiantly is as *a record of an attempt at making a movie*. This is the secret of bad movies that are good to watch. They have a kind of holographic quality, showing you the attempt at a thing as well as the thing itself, because the thing itself is so transparent that it cannot hide the attempt. In any film, an especially savvy audience member can perceive the attempt—can guess at the mechanisms Stanley Kubrick used to create his signature tracking shots, can understand that some of Terry Gilliam's genius lies in how well he uses a fisheye lens. But even *semi*-savvy viewers of bad film can perceive a failed attempt at a movie, can see what Wood or Wiseau or Bert I. Gordon were going for, the nature of their endeavor and how it compares to others' successes, and can follow the record of their failure.

The most enjoyable bad movies fail not just due to general incompetence but because of obvious peccadilloes: James Nguyen's fixation on Hitchcock (*Birdemic, Replica*), David Prior's fetish for not-quite-military stories (*Deadly Prey, Killzone*), Neil Breen's messiah complex (any of them). Wood's oeuvre was mostly lurid and exploitative, but *Plan 9* was a love letter to the movies he most adored. Repeated viewings show that love through the *record* of his *attempt* to do them justice. His peccadilloes charm and satisfy even as the execution of his ideas pratfalls. It's part of why *Plan 9* remains so watchable when other bad movies of its era bore and annoy. Wood wanted to succeed with a product he loved, where so many B-picture makers in the 50s just wanted to churn out the product.

Wood's affection does not make *Plan 9 from Outer Space* good. No force on earth could accomplish such a task. It's a good record, but not a good film. And the reasons why are abundant.

(4) CATEGORY

The qualities that make a good movie have been catalogued and debated exhaustively elsewhere. Whole libraries exist to explain how movies are good. But what makes a bad movie, how and why a film goes wrong—that's not studied so often. *Plan 9 from Outer Space* winds up being a useful exemplar for this question, and could be, perhaps, *the* exemplar from which a lesson plan for bad film can arise.

Tolstoy claimed that every unhappy family is unhappy in its own way. By the same logic, bad movies could go wrong in a thousand unique ways. But, after study, I've determined that Tolstoy does not apply here. Bad movies generally move in one of a handful of tracks:

1) Cynical trash. These movies are made entirely for profit, and bear no interest in art. Some big movies like *Battleship* lie here, but the similarities bear out all the way down to straight-to-video nonsense like *Samurai Cop II*. The main quality that distinguishes these movies is how obvious it is that *no one*, no actor, crewman, or creator, cares whether there's anything artistically sound about the film. *Everyone* is there for a paycheck. You might think of Michael Bay movies, but they demonstrate real craft;[13] his many imitators are closer to the mark.

2) Missing link. Movies are a team effort, generally requiring the work of dozens or hundreds. If just one of those cogs is out of alignment, the movie will be less-than. If the cog is large enough, the whole movie falls apart. Kevin Spacey is grossly miscast in *The Shipping News*, which makes the movie fail to cohere, since it's nearly a character study. The Russos don't direct anything but action particularly well, so a good deal of *Captain America: The Winter Soldier* feels impersonal and dim. The acting, writing, and production values are all there, but the angles and the proliferation of shakycam make the movie annoying to watch.

3) Movies that ought to work but don't. Attempted blockbusters go here to die. The biggest and best example is *Waterworld*, which had all the

[13] Tony Zhou of Every Frame a Painting proved this to me in 2014, and since then, I've gone about proving it to as many others as possible. Watch his video about "Bayhem" on YouTube and you just might be convinced, too.

money it could possibly have needed, plenty of star power, and an interesting premise. But it's an awful movie, as thin and weak as a seedling. Baz Luhrmann's *Australia* should have been a sweeping epic, a generous slice of awesome, and instead, no one has any fun, especially not the audience.

4) Poor photocopies. There's a species of straight-to-video movies called "mockbusters" that capitalize on looking similar to contemporary hits in the DVD rack. *Transmorphers* (*Transformers*), *Atlantic Rim* (*Pacific Rim*), *Android Cop* (…), you get the idea. Some filmmakers do this a little less blatantly and cynically, gathering up a few ideas in vogue and slapping a movie together, whether due to lack of imagination or the desire to be part of a zeitgeist. It never works. Inspiration and originality are always better than deliberate cribbing.

5) Auteur incompetence. This category has a very distinct pattern: a single filmmaker takes on every aspect of production, writing/producing/directing/starring/distributing/etc., and winds up in over his head to such a degree that the movie is a complete wreck. The photo negative of Orson Welles' achievement with *Citizen Kane*. Kings of bad film (Tommy Wiseau, Neil Breen) live here.

These categories can overlap. The Golan-Globus producing team made a lot of cynical trash, but plenty of it ought to have worked: they threw money, time, and talent at their projects, if not always in correct proportions, and every so often their ideas were actually good. Missing-link movies and movies that ought to work often overlap in the saddest ways. A great cast can be given terrible direction (the Star Wars prequels), or a good script can be edited to death. Kids' movies like *Boss Baby* are both cynical trash and poor photocopies.

Wood shows all the signs of no. 5: sheer, unshared incompetence. In his early work, he is enthusiastically in charge of everything about the movie, and everything about the movie goes wrong. His later work leans closer to cynical trash, but *Plan 9* is not a photocopy of anything, it doesn't have just one missing link, and there's not a single molecule of coulda-been-a-contender within it. It's all Wood's work, earnestly done, and it's all bad.

In *Plan 9*, Wood assembles a set of attributes for bad movies just as emergent as the common attributes of good movies: bad takes, cheap sets and props, terrible acting, witless writing, discontinuity, poor editing, inexpert framing, inappropriate lighting, illogical structure, and unintentional comedy. Many or most of these elements exist in all bad movies, although the last is possibly the most essential.

(5) MECHANISM

My very favorite thing in *Plan 9* is a line of Paula's:

```
                    PAULA
The saucers are up there. And the cemetery's
 out there. But I'll be locked up in there.
```

Free of context, this line communicates no more or less information than it does in the film. I think Paula's trying to say that despite nearby dangers, there (↑) and there (→), she'll be safe there (←), in the house. But the line is *so* badly written, from its broader intention of contributing to the screenplay and thus the story of *Plan 9 from Outer Space*, down to its nuts and bolts, the words it uses, that I cannot be sure. It's so badly written that it leaps out of the television at me every time I watch the film. It's so badly written that I cannot conceive of taking seriously, even for one moment, the film that contains a line like this. I always expect someone—Peter Bogdanovich, maybe—to stride onto the set in front of Paula and Jeff bellowing "Cut, cut, cut—can't we tweak that a little?" Someone, anyone, please interfere with the existence of this line spoken onto celluloid in the Year of Our Lord 1956. Undo it. Unmake it. Otherwise the very endeavor of cinema is in question, shaken at its foundations, because a crew full of living human beings could allow this line to be uttered and not simply walk away in resignation; because Wood could write this line, hear it delivered, and think "yes" rather than "no, no, a thousand times no." The existence of this line casts doubt on the artistic endeavors of all of us, like a vast and terrifying umbrella *de* bad art, shading our dreams from the sun.

Why is this my favorite part, this nadir of badness? Why is this terribly written and not-wonderfully-delivered line a source of delight rather than despair?

The mechanism inside me that loves bad movies is responsible, but I do not know how that mechanism functions, when it was built, nor what it does to transform bad art into joy. Paula's "there" line makes me sit up and notice, and even rewind to hear it again. I do the same thing for particularly well-said lines in *good* movies, for moments when an actor's craft shines brightly. Does it make any sense that I enjoy very good and very bad art in almost the same way—with delight, engagement, analysis, and repeat viewings?

No more than it makes sense to enjoy bad movies in the first place, I guess. Especially if I'm enjoying them without condescension in my heart.[14]

Anyway, this awful line may be my favorite part of *Plan 9* for its extraordinary vapidity, but it's hardly the only terrible moment in the film. I'll talk about many more individual moments in Part II, but for now, let's look at a scene that simply contradicts itself.

After a montage that juxtaposes stock footage of the military with the actions of Colonel Edwards and voiceover from Criswell explaining what's (meant to be) going on, Edwards has a conversation with an Army captain. It purports to be about firing missiles at the UFOs both men have just seen. The majority of the conversation only makes sense if both men acknowledge that their target is real UFOs.

CAPTAIN

Quite a sight, wasn't it, sir?

EDWARDS

A sight I'd rather not be seeing.

CAPTAIN

Are you worried about them, sir?

---

[14] More on this later.

EDWARDS
Well, they must have a reason for their visits.

CAPTAIN
Visits? Well, that would indicate visitors! Are big guns the usual way of welcoming visitors?

EDWARDS
We haven't always fired at them.

CAPTAIN
Oh?

But at the tail end of the scene:

CAPTAIN
Oh, this is a training maneuver, sir. We only did a little practice firing at the clouds.

The line invalidates the entire scene, and Col. Edwards's stated role as the man "in charge of saucer field activities," and even the montage and voiceover that preceded. It's been suggested[15] that the captain says the line sarcastically, knowing that he has to play along with the omerta laid down by the "upper echelon." But if it is sarcasm, it's amazingly subtle, in a film that does not otherwise acknowledge the existence of subtlety as a concept. The actor's performance does not suggest sarcasm to me. Instead, it seems like he relieves his own anxiety about these uncertain "visitors" by repeating that he was only participating in a training maneuver.

[15] By Rob Craig in *Ed Wood, Mad Genius*.

Why on earth was the scene written this way?[16]

The captain's last line belongs to a scene in which Edwards knows the UFOs are real and the captain does not, but that isn't the scene we just witnessed. Most of the dialogue belongs to a scene in which Edwards and the captain candidly discuss something they're not supposed to admit they saw, but the conclusion to that scene isn't the one in the film. The result is a Moebius strip of a scene, one in which two approaches do not cohere into one meaning. This move would almost ascend into an intellectual puzzle, except that it's the result of idiotic screenwriting rather than a genuine intention of unsettling the audience.

Often, for exactly the opposite of this reason, experimental art reads as bad art, especially for mainstream audiences.[17] Inconsistency reads as error, rather than a purposeful disruption of audience expectations. Consistency

---

[16] Remember what I said in my author's note about the differences between the screenplay and the finished film? Well, this scene is written very differently than the filmed version. It's a lot shorter, so the back-and-forth about the saucers doesn't have the chance to contradict itself quite so much.

CAPTAIN
Do you suppose Washington will also deny this "rumor"?
COLONEL
It was Washington that gave this fire order.
CAPTAIN
Ten to one the files read "Training maneuvers."
[pace change]
Looks like we beat them off again, sir.
COLONEL
What are they? What do they want? Where do they come from? Where do they go?
CAPTAIN
They, sir? Who? Why this is a training maneuver, sir. We only did a little practice firing at the clouds.
COLONEL
Wonder what their next move'll be.

All punctuation Wood's. The scene still doesn't make sense, because it's *still* unclear when and whether the captain is being sarcastic, while Col. Edwards mostly speaks as if the captain isn't even there. Also, Criswell's voiceover is not written into the screenplay at all. But this version is a little less crazymaking than the final film.

[17] The most interesting book I read about Wood was Rob Craig's *Ed Wood, Mad Genius*. He claims that Wood was a brilliant outsider artist whose films rely on Brechtian and Absurdist theatre ideas. I think he is dead wrong, because Occam's razor applies (either Wood was secretly one of the most thoughtful and best-read filmmakers in Hollywood at the time, forging a unique vision during the worst decade of the century to do so, or he was simply short on money and talent), and because theatre and cinema theories are more incompatible than they seem. But Craig does shore up my point here, that if you are *very* determined to read bad art as experimental art or vice versa, it's possible to do so.

is safe and clean and easy to digest, and experimentalists do not prize these qualities.

When I read or see something experimental and avant-garde, it's my job as a critic to work out whether the artist's ambitions make sense, not whether the end result makes sense *to me*. (It's a hair's breadth away from considering artist intent, but an important hair.) Sometimes I can't understand what the art is doing, but I'm aware that it has consistency and internal logic. "She's clearly up to something," is my best praise for experimental art I can't penetrate. An inner integrity to the art conveys meaning, even without a message I can interpret.

One of my favorite tales to tell in the classroom is itself a teaching story. My mother, a professor specializing in early modern poetry and translation, sometimes taught Shakespeare to college sophomores. Sometimes she assigned *Coriolanus*, which is rarely taught or performed, being a bit weird, and violent, and stark, and Roman. My mother assigned the play knowing her students would hate it, because they always do. She told them ahead of time to try and read with an open mind. The next class, she asked them to tell her the reasons they hated *Coriolanus* (again, they always did; there were always answers to this question), and she wrote them on the board. Then she went through all these reasons and demonstrated that nearly all of them arose not from flaws in the play, but from unmet expectations on the part of the student. The student expected X, Y, and Z from a Shakespeare play, and instead got H, Q, and M. The play was not bad; the student was annoyed that the play didn't do what he thought it would.

The average reader[18] dislikes almost nothing more than having his expectations upended. It makes him hostile, because all of a sudden, the world is no longer well-ordered and easily understood. Possibilities open up, and he hasn't thought of them, and that means he's unsafe, out of control, a rube in the big city, lost in the forest.

After this exercise, few of my mother's students liked *Coriolanus* much better, but most of them respected it more. She had to demonstrate what the play was actually doing, within its own little parabola, and how

[18] Emphasis on "average," whether widely read or not. Many readers, of all stripes, enjoy having their expectations upended. But a hell of a lot of people read cozy mysteries.

those actions were off-target only in light of the reader's expectations, not in light of what the play meant and messaged. Its violation of audience expectations is part of its genius, part of its experimentalism: a feature, not a bug.

Seeing any violation of expectations as a bug is how audiences close their minds. It's how we get homogenous art. It's how work that dares gets written off as work that fails.[19]

This cluster of ideas brings me back to bad film again and again. Few good movies have the capacity to surprise me, particularly in contemporary American cinema, but bad movies are *bottomlessly* surprising. They violate my expectations over and over. They fail to conform to standards so rigidly established they might as well be law. They *fail*, generally; this is unfortunate, but it doesn't deter the pleasure I take in them. I delight in how carelessly a Z film tosses off the shackles of linear storytelling, three-act structure, rational casting, and a coherent visual style. *Plan 9* does all of this, which is part of what makes it so much fun to watch. What will happen in the next 10 minutes? No idea. A stock footage montage, for no reason? Sure, okay. Recast one of the most distinctive actors of the 20th century midway through? All righty. Guy in a cowboy hat appears out of nowhere to save Paula from the monster? I can get on board with that. Didn't see it coming, but whatever. At least it's not another Dark Night of the Soul.[20]

In a good film, broadly predicting the next 10 or 30 or 50 minutes is like predicting the weather in southern California. *It'll be sunny*. There are variations, but mostly, trust me, it's gonna look like this. I find joy in the chaos of bad movies. Others find greater joy in the comfort of predictable character arcs and sound plot resolutions. This is fine; but you can't talk me out of the *uses* of bad art, the ways in which it illuminates good art, keeps it honest.

---

[19] This is not to say that work that fails should be regarded generously as work that dares (as Craig does, bless him). Bad art should not be excused with a flippant "oh, it's experimental." Sometimes this is case-by-case; I will defend *Death Bed: The Bed That Eats* as both bad *and* experimental. For now, restrict my conclusion to: meritorious experimental art is often mistaken for bad art, and it is not.

[20] Here, narrowly, Craig and I agree: "Unconventional film tends to distance an audience expecting generic, predictable entertainment, even as it attracts those who seek something challenging and different." From *Ed Wood, Mad Genius*.

(6) ENTHUSIASM

I've chosen to write at such great length about bad movies in part because of the above: the wonder of their unpredictability, my belief in them as teaching tools, the scale and spectrum they help to define between their efforts and movies that are excellent or just mediocre. I know, too, that I have a high tolerance for the otherwise painful parts of bad movies. My reaction to discontinuity, visible boom mikes, and inept screenwriting is usually mirth, not annoyance.

However, some things do get to me. There are few examples in *Plan 9* of issues I can't tolerate,[21] but here's a pretty well-known one from another movie: in *Over the Top* (1987), the main character is inconsistently referred to as either "Hawk" or "Hawks." There is no excuse for this kind of mistake. A director or an assistant director or a script supervisor or even the actor who played Hawk(s) should have stopped the scene to correct the mistake, every single time. That they didn't means no one cared enough about such basic filmmaking integrity as *the main character's correct name* to solve the problem, neither then and there nor later, in editing, in ADR, ever. Other things about *Over the Top* crack me up (that it's structured like a romantic comedy, except the meet-cute is between a man and his estranged son; that it's wall-to-wall arm-wrestling for the final half-hour), but that mistake just pisses me off. It indicates that no one gave a damn. On a film set, someone, anyone, should always give a damn.

When a movie is cynical, when the filmmakers have whoomped up this product and put everyone to work to make something meaningless, not for pleasure or ambition but solely for profit, I never have a good time. A huge swath of direct-to-video movies qualifies, with titles like *Oblivion* (1994) and *Merlin: The Return* (2000). Charles Band made piles of them, mostly as producer. These movies are insulting. They wasted the time of everyone involved in production and they waste the audience's time, too. They exist on the premise that it's easier to make and sell meaningless crap than meaningful crap, and I cannot withstand this idea. It's wasteful. Good unproduced screenplays are inexpensive and plentiful! You have the resources to make something with costumes and special effects and actors, and you make *this*? To hell with you.

---

[21] See pp. 42-43 for one.

But a lack of cynicism—this element makes watchable so many awful films, including *Plan 9 from Outer Space*. Wood loved movies, he loved Hollywood, he loved monsters and aliens, and he put everything he had into this single project. That it came out the way it did reflects one critic's assessment of the film as "a triumph of will over talent."[22] It's a lousy movie because Wood was a lousy writer and director. But he *loved* what he was doing, and that enthusiasm oozes from every frame of *Plan 9*, for better or worse. Earnest efforts at filmmaking are almost never a waste of time.

The naïveté *Plan 9* displays about its own flaws and faults presses its audience to feel a kind of incredulous affection. *It really believes it's good*, the audience thinks. *It really believes it's doing well.* This is sweet, like tiny kids playing soccer is sweet, as they trip over each other and bumble vaguely in the direction of the gently rolling ball and sometimes wander off to the edges of the field. Wood not knowing that he could be doing any better lets us love him and his creation. If he *elected* not to do any better—choosing to cheap out, when he had available the option of a better script and fewer gaffes—that would make the film unenjoyable. I would be angry at him for wasting resources, rather than feeling endeared to his incompetence.

Again, viewing *Plan 9* as a successful record of the *attempt* to make a film is much more emotionally profitable than viewing it as a failed film. As a record, *Plan 9* reflects a dedicated filmmaker with unique ideas, one unconstrained by genre boundaries or typical narrative arcs. This filmmaker surrounded himself with flash-in-the-pan weirdos and unlikely patrons, and from those ingredients, cooked up a stew of inadequate flavor but unusual complexity. Such an attempt may be gently ribbed, but never dismissed as meaningless. Making things we love is perhaps the deepest human endeavor, only one notch above storytelling as the most powerful way to keep ourselves from the void. Wood genuinely loved *Plan 9*, and so do I.

I love the airplane cockpit scenes, filmed in a set that would have to vastly improve to meet the condition "bare minimum." I love that the police lieutenant explains that many UFO sightings don't include "a glow" by saying "well, haven't you heard?" as if UFO sightings are changing

---

[22] This phrase was spoken by a male voice in the early minutes of *Flying Saucers Over Hollywood: The Plan 9 Companion*. I don't know who it was—presumably one of the many interviewees in the film.

hemlines or developments in a showy trial. I love that there is no sensible universe in which Bela Lugosi's character's wife looks like Vampira, in death or in life, and yet there she lurks. I love the proliferant fog in the cemetery set, which exists to no purpose. I love with all my heart the actress who comments on Lugosi's character's death, "First his wife, then he." There may never be an actress with worse line delivery, though we search high and low. She has no conviction, no confidence, and no interest in what she says. She is awful, failing even at *trying* to act, and for this reason I love her dearly.

In a good film, she would have been replaced. (But then, in a good film, she wouldn't have asked a deeply pointless question about the virtue of burial vs. crypt.) Someone would have recast either Vampira or Lugosi to make their marriage more plausible. The cockpit set would have actual equipment in it. The film's plot would be comprehensible from early on, and there would be no sequences of stock footage. Characters wouldn't run in circles and scenes wouldn't contradict themselves. A good film would give us so much less.

(7) EYE

The list of flaws in *Plan 9* can go on at enormous length. My point is not to ridicule the film—I love it too much to do that with genuine disdain in my heart—but to demonstrate how easy it is to locate and name *easily fixable* flaws in the film. It's a movie that brazenly shows what not to do at every decision point, from casting all the way to editing. And its flaws are so evident, so apparent, that the viewer doesn't need a film degree to see what's going wrong.

While drafting this section I watched *Birds of Prey*, a 2020 film about the DC Comics character Harley Quinn et al. It was so seriously flawed that I didn't enjoy it. A handful of my friends had seen it earlier in the year and lauded it to me. This has happened repeatedly in my adult life, but I was particularly surprised when it happened with *Birds of Prey*.

I *do* have a film degree, which honed and lent experience to a native talent for film analysis. What I saw in *Birds* was:

- Flamboyant voiceover tying together unconventional plot sequencing, which should have worked but made the film lose momentum repeatedly
- A screenwriter who didn't understand that the best part of an ensemble film is when the ensemble is assembled, not the lead-up to that event
- Action sequences that cribbed from copies of copies of interesting action sequences
- Music choices that started out unique and devolved into cliché
- Art direction so immoderate that, in the climax, the set read like a set instead of a genuine environment of any kind
- A miscast Ewan McGregor

I'm certain that most of my friends did not see most of this. For some, the action scenes felt comfortable instead of tired. The sequencing reminded them favorably of *Pulp Fiction* instead of reading as pointless, and it distracted them from the thin plot. Margot Robbie's extraordinary talent hid the weaknesses of the film she carried.

These failures are not me being picky, nor my friends being blind. They're hidden in plain sight. Movies in this decade click along so rapidly and appealingly, with a plethora of pleasing textures and interesting colors and distracting motion, that the untrained audience member is too dazzled to perceive that they are often watching crap. I loved *Birds of Prey*'s costumes and it was plainly a well-financed film; the aroma of studio money disguises the reek of studio shit pretty well. But not perfectly. I have a very good nose.

The point: it takes effort and training to perceive the failures of the average studio film. It takes a ton of hours in a dark room watching shadows. It is *hard*. Studios do everything possible to disguise these failures. But filmmakers like Edward D. Wood, Jr. make undisguisably bad movies. Their flaws are visible to anyone with one eye and half a brain (except, evidently, Wood himself).

The more obvious the failure, the more valuable the film to cinema students of all kinds—makers, critics, buffs. If they can pick out poor transitions as they happen, and notice the difference between film stocks when stock footage appears, they might be able to spot more subtle flaws in more legitimate movies. If I hadn't seen *Gigli*[23] fail completely at flamboyant voiceover, I might not have noticed that *Birds of Prey*'s doesn't hit the mark. If I hadn't suffered through Jason Beghe as Hank Rearden in the second installment of *Atlas Shrugged*,[24] I wouldn't have understood why McGregor's performance was irritating instead of quirky.

As I watch bad film, my eye for film improves. I can discern so much more about what's in the frame of a good film, for example, by observing what's in the frame of a bad film. There's a yawning gulf between bad framing and unimaginative framing, but you can't really see it until you see enough of the former. If you've ever gone from an average American film to a good French film, you know what I mean. The gulf there is between unimaginative framing and innovative framing, and it yawns just as widely.

Bad film is much more plentiful than film objectively good enough to be taught, and I posit that bad film has even more to teach. *Plan 9*'s flaws are a decent sampling of how film can go wrong, but there are scores more flaws out there that other movies have explored. In the films of Coleman Francis, nothing happens. Neil Breen's work has unignorable tics—objects dropping to the ground, shots of feet—that fail to create meaning through repetition. Some films are poorly lit, others have painful musical numbers, others are weird patchworks of popular ideas. But every item in this paragraph is a useful point of reference for an aspiring filmmaker or critic. *This is what could go wrong. This is how to recognize what isn't working. This problem crops up in mediocre film, too, but here it's big enough to see.* It's hard to show someone what the work of a good boom operator looks like. It's incredibly easy to point out a bad one.

Bad film also fascinates with the *range* of its flaws. Why is it that Wood can light a scene, but can't block one? Why do so many bad directors get eyelines right, but framing wrong? How can Coleman Francis so consistently forget to have anything *happen* in his movies? "What were they thinking?" is not the most useful question about bad movies. Far from it.

---

[23] Not recommended. Painful in how it fails.

[24] Also not recommended. I usually love vanity projects, and the first one (2011) was kind of an interesting mess, but *Atlas Shrugged II* (2012) is negative fun.

The more I pick apart bad film, the more there is to study and understand. Everything in them grants me insight on the labor of movie-making—the risk of it, the scads of individual vibrating electrons that have to unite in purpose to create a usable molecule.

Since bad movies like *Plan 9* are so often successful records of an attempt to make a good movie, they contain valuable archival information. Like the notebooks of a novelist. Except the novelist in this case is not a single creator, but the conglomerate artistic endeavor of filmmaking. Bad film is a long, entertaining, wearying record of that endeavor's failed sorties. The only way to properly admire the success is to witness the failure.

(8) RIFF

On my right bicep is a colorful tattoo of Tom Servo, one of the robot characters from the television show *Mystery Science Theater 3000*, which ran on various networks from 1988 to 1999. The premise of the show was an elaborate frame for a pretty simple idea: let's make fun of bad movies. Tom Servo, along with another robot named Crow and a human companion, Joel (1988-1993) or Mike (1993-1999), are forced by bad bosses to watch these stinkers, and they avoid despair by cracking jokes, or "riffing," on the movies' risible qualities. The creators of *MST3K* mostly continue to do this work in new formats, whether Michael J. Nelson's RiffTrax, Joel Hodgson's two Netflix seasons of a revived *MST3K* starring Jonah Ray, or Trace Beaulieu and Frank Conniff's live touring show, The Mads.

I don't know for sure, but I think part of the reason these men keep doing the same weird job 20+ years after the original show ended is because of how specialized it is, which leads to audience demand (no matter how niche) that can't be met by very many people. Riffing seems a lot easier than it is. The concentration of jokes has to be high, one every seven to 10 seconds, and that energy has to keep up for a movie's running time, around 5,400 seconds. That's more than 500 jokes. Decent jokes.

Beyond the per capita problem, there's a special breed of integrity in what *MST3K* did with its films that's even harder to duplicate. Very rarely did the riffers condescend to the film at issue, or take cheap shots at it, or insult it. Sometimes this did happen; comments about Joe Don Baker's weight,[25] for instance, or about a female actor's annoying voice.[26] But most often, the *MST3K* writers made jokes that met the movie where it lived, that engaged with the movie instead of punching down at it. Imitators have tried to do it the other way, just hurling insults for 90 minutes, and it does not work. Joking about a movie's plot (or lack thereof),[27] or about ideas presented in its dialogue, gives the viewer some *substance* to laugh about, a hook to hang humor on, as opposed to just, say, mocking bad special effects. The latter is obvious and represents shallow, fleeting engagement with the film. *MST3K*'s work with film shows almost universal respect for the endeavor of filmmaking, even if that respect drops to minimal levels for certain movies.

An example: in *Outlaw of Gor*, characters often say "Where the hell am I?" and the riffers always respond "You're the hell here." The joke is simple, but the repetition makes it funnier, and points out ably that the script is repetitive. They could have made fun of the sidekick's dorky glasses, but that's a bully move. Digging into what the screenplay does wrong is an *analytical* move.

Many fans of *MST3K* go on to be fans of bad movies, your author included. The danger in going gaily from the satire to the real thing lies in failing to understand the mechanism of *MST3K*'s engagement with film and perceiving only that it's fun to laugh at bad movies. Make no mistake: the writers of *MST3K* know as much about film as scholars, as historians, as producers and directors. They know what it is and isn't to make a movie. Sometimes the riffs gesture toward this thesis of mine, that bad film is profoundly instructive in the ways of good film: noting the use of the grip truck as a stunt vehicle in *Werewolf* or a very pointed continuity problem in *Space Mutiny*. Of course, sometimes they just play word games and build extended jokes about Ron Howard's *Willow*.

---

[25] Evidently Baker made a rude public statement about how *Mitchell* got riffed, so the crew did not hold back when they riffed *Final Justice*.

[26] They're not very nice to Kathy Ireland in *Alien from L.A.*, but, even with my most feminist hat on, her voice is *awful* in that movie. A minor character in *Tormented* also gets this treatment, which I excuse a little less.

[27] Cf *The Castle of Fu Manchu*.

Irresponsible and mean-hearted entertainers have used the *MST3K* model to fling mud at movies without the depth of understanding the original riffers held. They think the value of *MST3K* lies in tearing down the failed work of incompetent filmmakers—in shaming them. No. The value is in analysis. Comedy is best when it analyzes, not when it skims and pokes along the surface of something. Jerry Seinfeld's observational humor does not have the intellectual durability of George Carlin's excoriation of societal mores. *MST3K* must analyze the badness of a film before riffing it, and that's why the concept works without relying on cruelty (for the most part). Their process *opens* the film, where mocking *closes* it.

But because the riffs are breezy and the show is an inexpensive Midwestern creation, it looks like easy work, making fun of movies so bad the jokes seem to happen of their own accord. So folks who fancy themselves cultural critics begin ridiculing, in the model but not the spirit of *MST3K*, and the whole discourse of cinema studies suffers. It's too bad. The legacy of *MST3K* could be its commitment to sorting through the sludge at the bottom of the barrel, surfacing with phenomenal examples of the weirdest and worst of what cinema has to offer.[28] I would not trade the hours I've spent watching *MST3K* for an afternoon with Ingmar Bergman or Alfred Hitchcock. I'm positive I learned more from the riffs.

Where the rubber meets the road: there exists a RiffTrax for *Plan 9 from Outer Space*. It's funny. Conveniently, there's a good example of unkind ridicule in it: a running joke about Bela Lugosi's morphine addiction. It's beneath them, and it stings badly, especially when held against Tim Burton's tender portrayal of the same issue in *Ed Wood*. Otherwise, it's a solid riff, pointing out Lt. Harper's hilariously unsafe gestures with his prop gun, the evocative shape of the aliens' mother ship, and multiple ways in which Wood cheaped out on production, like the "police car" outside the "station" and the bad cockpit set. If you missed how ungracefully Wood switches between studio shots and day-for-night location shots, RiffTrax has your back. And they expose some of the illogic in the script, like the "Solaronite" speech and Criswell's opening monologue.

---

[28] Some films, like *Manos: The Hands of Fate*, might have been permanently lost if not for the *MST3K* treatment. A dubious reward, perhaps.

RiffTrax does not get the last word on *Plan 9*. Edward D. Wood, Jr. does. The movie has stuck around not because it's hated or mocked, but because it's loved—because of its flaws, I wager, not in spite of them.

(9) AGGREGATE

What I've learned from bad movies, I've learned from the preponderance of them. Patterns appear, like the degree to which they lean on inflated stakes and exploitation, or the amount of time spent on driving and parking. Lumps and bumps appear in all kinds of movies; the other day I spotted a mid-scene cut in the Coens' *True Grit*, a masterpiece. But the lessons of bad movies exist most usefully in aggregate. That means examining a single bad film or a small handful of them is not necessarily the best way to learn the lessons within them.

This is true for good film, too. You can't learn everything you need to know about filmmaking just from *Citizen Kane*. Again, you have to be an omnivore, absorbing as much as you can from as many different levels and styles of artwork as you can. You have to go everywhere, and you have to remember where you've been every time you sit down to work.

That said, if you were to select just one bad movie to try and learn from, *Plan 9 from Outer Space* is a top choice. It's unofficially considered the *Citizen Kane* of bad movies, after all. Although I'm not sure the reason for that is especially well-grounded, I'd posit that it's a kind of direct oppositional force to *Citizen Kane*. Everything *Kane* does right, *Plan 9* does wrong. It has a very deep bench, in terms of the flaws it offers up and how plainly they appear. I have learned from so many bad movies—well into the hundreds—but *Plan 9* is the granddaddy of them all.

The only way to assess a single bad movie thoroughly enough to learn from it is to perform an exegesis: an exhaustive analysis, scene by scene. So that is what I shall do.

PLAN 9
FROM
OUTER
SPACE
with
BELA LUGOSI
VAMPIRA
LYLE TALBOT
A J. Edward Reynolds Production
Produced and Directed by
Edward D. Wood, Jr.
3
58-294

II: EXEGESIS

WE OPEN ON **CRISWELL PREDICTS**, A TITLE CARD THAT LIKELY visually echoes Criswell's regular TV show.[29] The speech Criswell, whose record of untrue predictions has been well-covered elsewhere, gives, is so extraordinary that I must reproduce it in full.[30]

CRISWELL

Greetings, my friend. We are all interested in the future, for that is where you and I are going to spend the rest of our lives. And remember, my friend, future events such as these will affect you in the future. You are interested in the unknown, the mysterious, the unexplainable. That is why you are here. And now, for the first time, we are bringing to you the full story of what happened on that fateful day. We are giving you all the evidence, based only on the secret testimonies of the miserable souls who survived this

---

[29] Criswell's daily (!) show ran from 1953 to 1961. All episodes have been lost.

[30] Per Mason (1990), Criswell wrote this himself. I'm skeptical, because it reads so much like Wood, and there are other errors in Mason's editorial work in that book. However, none of Criswell's lines appear in the screenplay. Could he have written his entire voiceover? Most likely to me is that Wood wrote it in post-production, but my research doesn't say. One source indicated that Criswell's show always opened with those three lines: "Greetings, my friend [...] will affect you in the future." I don't quite believe this, because the lines are so often quoted as an example of Wood's bad writing, and surely someone with a memory of Criswell's show would have corrected this misapprehension.

```
terrifying ordeal. The incidents, the places—
my friend, we cannot keep this a secret any
longer. Let us punish the guilty. Let us
reward the innocent. My friend, can your heart
stand the shocking facts about grave robbers
from outer space?
```

It's an excellent blend of inane, circular, and alarmist, very clearly read from a script out of frame (you can see Criswell's eyes move), with delivery as unique and risible as William Shatner's. Aspects of the speech do not cohere to the film that follows; for instance, "what happened on that fateful day," when the fateful events took place over a series of days or potentially weeks, and "punish the guilty… reward the innocent," when the guilty are all dead, aliens, or dead aliens. Not a stellar beginning, to demonstrate inconsistency before the movie even begins.

Next come the credits, which vary between words "carved" on a gravestone and words projected against a photo of a cemetery. The variation has no logic. The theme music for *Plan 9 from Outer Space* is sort of dumb, thudding and dramatic and simplistic, but it's also immediately recognizable and sets the tone well.[31] Wood's credit arrives in a clap of thunder and is styled as "Written-Produced-Directed" against a black sky full of stars.

The next six minutes compose most of Bela Lugosi's work in the film. Criswell narrates as a small collection of mourners, including Lugosi, stands around an open grave. It appears to be midday. No diegetic[32] dialogue. The "old man" (Lugosi) has lost his wife. Her death came "suddenly and without warning" despite Lugosi's obvious age. We cut, thrice, to a pair of gravediggers sitting on the ground doing nothing in approximately the same kind of landscape and lighting.

[31] The music from *Plan 9* is all library music, the auditory equivalent to stock footage. *Nightmare of Ecstasy* claims the main title is Alexander Mosolov's *Iron Foundry*, but it is not. Music writer Paul Mandell traced the full story of the film's music for *Film Score Monthly* in 1996: https://web.archive.org/web/20101013003604/http://sammel-surium.heimat.eu/soundtracks/P9FSM.html

[32] "Diegetic" means it originates and exists within the world of the film, where "non-diegetic" means the opposite. Diegetic music would be music that comes from a visible radio or performer, where non-diegetic music is, for instance, the Imperial March in *The Empire Strikes Back*.

CRISWELL

It was when the gravediggers started their task that strange things began to take place.

Yet instead of showing these strange things, we cut to a plane in the sky. Screenwriting lesson: do not set up something you don't knock down. The audience has a short memory. If you say something as anticipatory as Criswell's line, you have to follow it up, preferably then and there. Chekhov's gun does not apply in B pictures.

The plane, as it turns out, provides an establishing shot. Cut to the apparent inside of a cockpit, which has no equipment at all. Just a clipboard tacked to one wall and a circular chart, likely a flight computer, tacked to the other. Two men, dressed in pilots' uniforms, sit in a two-shot. The man on the left has a microphone for a two-way radio strapped to his chest. Both men have in front of them half-circles of plywood attached to poles, intended, somehow, to be steering devices for the "plane." The pilot, on the right, is Jeff; the copilot, with the radio, is Danny.

A little unconvincing, uninteresting dialogue passes between the men, and then a commotion of light and sound interrupts them. Outside the window floats a flying saucer, on visible piano wire,[33] before a background of painted clouds. Nothing about it looks remotely convincing as a special effect.

A female flight attendant, Edith, joins them. The saucer moves away, out of frame.

```
                    EDITH
          What in the world...

                    DANNY
       That's nothing from this world.
```

The copilot communicates a mayday into the radio. My understanding goes that "mayday" should be reserved for extreme emergencies, not for unthreatening appearances of UFOs, but he says it anyway. The saucer flings from left to right across a couple of shots with different drawn backgrounds, and then, in a process shot, sinks into the photograph of the Los Angeles cemetery that appeared in the credits. Again, none of this is convincing. The saucer wobbles like a toy.

Cut to the gravediggers. Aha! This must be a strange thing beginning to take place! Except the background of the gravediggers doesn't match the cemetery from the process shot where the UFO landed, and the cockpit scene was long enough to disconnect the viewer from the funeral, the gravediggers, and the supposed strange things. Wood attempts to make the connection through editing—juxtaposing the saucer, the cemetery, and the gravediggers. But editing fails to provide continuity when the shots contain no inherent similarities (lighting, perspective).

Throughout *Plan 9 from Outer Space*, Wood tries to depend on parataxis to connect one thing to another. Parataxis is a literary strategy that forces meaningful connections between disparate phrases or ideas merely by setting them next to each other. Samuel Beckett used it in *Not I*, stringing together many short, disconnected phrases to cast the spell of an idea rather

---

[33] Probably, per *Nightmare of Ecstasy*.

than stating it outright. David Markson uses parataxis boldly; some of his books are long lists of facts that only connect to each other cumulatively, over the course of many pages. He makes few traditional narrative connections, and instead leaves it up to the reader to determine what the small, disconnected units of meaning have in common with each other.

If Wood were being this obtuse on purpose, I'd call him a surrealist, lining up a series of shots that have little in common in order to make an artistic impression rather than tell a linear story. But that is not what's going on. Wood means for the two cemeteries he has put on screen thus far—the one with Lugosi and the one in the still photograph—to be just one. He means for the gravediggers to appear to be in the same place; the threefold cuts between the funeral scene and the gravediggers indicate that they're supposed to be nearby, watching the funeral. Shortly Wood will introduce a third cemetery, in a studio, and it, too, is meant to be the same place. The saucer that appeared near the plane cockpit connects to the omnicemetery, which connects to the gravediggers, who connect to the funeral. Supposedly.

Where Beckett and Markson are graceful with parataxis, Wood is clumsy. Mere juxtaposition doesn't provide enough consistency to help the audience understand the connections Wood attempts. The reason is wrapped up with the acceptable grammar of cinema, which was established a hundred years ago and has only been refined—not dramatically changed—since.

Three main elements establish consistency between shots in the audience's mind: lighting, location, and landmarks. Cutting from a scene with dim lighting to a scene with strong lighting leads an audience to believe you're cutting to a different *time* (night to day). Cutting from a location shot to a studio shot leads the audience to believe you're cutting to a different *place* (outside to inside). Cutting between places that have no recognizably similar landmarks makes the audience lose track of the characters' *movement*. The average moviegoer might not be able to explain this if asked, but editing consistency depends upon these three elements as basic premises. Keep your lighting consistent between shots that are meant to take place at the same time; keep the appearance of your location consistent between shots meant to occur in the same place; keep the landmarks clear in frame if you want the audience to know where the characters are and where they're going.

Many, many examples will come up between now and the end of this monograph of Wood misusing this basic grammar of consistency in *Plan 9 from Outer Space*. In each circumstance, it's useful to remember the three Ls.

The gravediggers think they hear something "sorta spooky-like" in, I remind you, a cemetery, and decide to leave without finishing their task, which is, I remind you, burying the old man's wife. Cut to mist rising against a black backdrop, with a dead tree and a portion of a structure in the foreground. It's unmistakably a studio shot, while the gravediggers are on location outdoors. Vampira emerges from the edge of the structure—cue dramatic violins—and, the editing suggests, advances on the gravediggers. The implication of danger exists based on nothing but editing proximity. The gravediggers and Vampira never appear in the same shot, and the locations and lighting are completely different.

Also, here's the first evidence of Wood's inability to block scenes logically: the gravediggers are walking *away* from supposedly covering *her* grave. Unless they walk in a circle, or she rose from the grave without them seeing her (??) and waited a little distance away to attack them, it makes no sense that they would meet her *approaching* them.

The gravediggers scream off-camera as Vampira raises her arms (in a medium shot, which is not as effective as a close-up would have been). Fade to black.

Later we learn that Vampira is meant to be the old man (Lugosi)'s recently deceased wife. This is not intuitive. She is clearly not of an age with him, and her appearance is extreme. "Wife" is no part of what that appearance communicates—not in 1959. The implication may be that her costume and makeup result from her ghoul-ness, from her zombified nature, rather than depicting how she appeared in life. We cannot know, as we have no basis for comparison, because we never saw her when she was alive. The appearance of the other ghouls is inconclusive in this regard; Tor looks the same except for white contact lenses, and with Lugosi it's difficult to draw a comparison given that he's played by two different actors once he's a ghoul. The fact that Vampira had to be recognizable as

Vampira in order to be an attraction for film audiences familiar with her TV show is certainly a piece of this puzzle, and it's one example of the film's backstage motivations resulting in onscreen confusion.

A lot of this information is to come. We in the audience don't even know she's a ghoul yet, and certainly we can't connect the existence of ghouls with the saucers. But that's my point: we see a scary woman, we see the gravediggers being put in jeopardy? maybe?, and we have no context for any of it. Just the editing, which juxtaposes all this without imparting much information and without making physical sense. I can put the pieces together after watching *Plan 9* multiple times, but the idea that the audience could have seen past all these leaps in logic to connect Vampira with Lugosi, and with the flying saucers, on the basis of *editing*, staggers me.

Cut to Lugosi leaving a small, unattractive ranch house while Criswell narrates about his grief. It's a pretty silly speech, and it makes Lugosi's tender acting seem overbaked. Also, he's wearing a caped coat in this scene, which sort of connects to Vampira's costume, but really just reminds the viewer of the actor's fame as Dracula rather than offering a sense of his character in *Plan 9 from Outer Space*.[34] (The fact that he never gets a name doesn't help.) He walks left, offscreen, and the film freezes. You can tell because the spindly tree in the center of the shot, previously tossed by the wind, stops moving, and because Lugosi's shadow remains on the lawn even as the sound effects of squealing brakes and a scream materialize, indicating that the owner of the shadow has come to some great harm.

Cut to stock footage of, apparently, an ambulance; a siren wails over the footage, but the writing on the back of the car is indistinct. Fade to black.

Fade up on a crypt the size of a child's playhouse, against the same stark backdrop as Vampira's "attack." Four people emerge from the playhouse crypt. Criswell reveals that this is the old man's funeral (at night?) and his . . . DEAD WIFE (cut to Vampira) is watching. Ah! Vampira is the dead wife! Wait, really?

The mourners are not the same mourners as at the wife's funeral. Two linger for a bad, expository conversation:

---

[34] Perhaps Wood meant to offer dual resonance—to connect to Vampira *and* to remind the audience of Dracula. But one of these references is in-film and the other is metatextual, and using one piece of costume to imply both is just confusing rather than efficient and/or winking.

WOMAN MOURNER

Tell me something. Why was his wife buried in the ground, and he sealed in a crypt?

MAN MOURNER

Something to do with family tradition. A superstition of some sort.

WOMAN MOURNER

Oh.

I do not have a satisfactory answer for why this matters. Maybe Wood thought the gravediggers on location vs. the playhouse crypt in a studio needed some kind of diegetic explanation. It really does not, or at least no more than any of the other inconsistencies apparent in this record of the film so far, and yet here is this dialogue, delivered by a not-that-bad actor and the Worst Actress in the World.[35] The Worst Actress in the World discovers the dead gravediggers, or really two mannequins dressed like the dead gravediggers, and screams.

We need to talk about time frame for a moment. Let's assume that the old man's funeral could have been put together in a week. Let's further assume that only a week passed between Vampira's death and the old man's walk into traffic. That would still mean the dead gravediggers had been lying there for two entire weeks without anyone a) noticing they were missing or b) noticing their rotting corpses. I think the idea is that these events happened right on top of each other, in a matter of days.[36] But that is even more unrealistic than the plot has been thus far. And it's a *logical* inconsistency, not a fantasy-based run of the imagination. Funerals take more than a day to plan. Despair like the old man's doesn't develop overnight. It's just not credible.

I write those words and then laugh at myself, laying out a reasonable argument for why something in *Plan 9 from Outer Space* is not credible.

[35] See p. 25 for further thoughts on this gal.

[36] In the screenplay, Larry the policeman says of the bodies, "Looks like they've been here a coupla days." So Wood did *attempt* to give us a time frame, but it didn't end up in the film. And it's still illogical.

But it matters that Wood handwaved his way through real-world logic even as he ignored bad framing and terrible performances and silly plot contrivances. Movies breathe and expire on the confidence viewers have in them, and ignoring the timeline of funerals and body decomposition erodes that confidence just as ably as a crummy UFO model on a visible bit of piano wire. What frustrates me about bad movies is not the cheapness of a film or the incompetence of its crew or actors, but choices like this timeline thing. Wood could have implemented any of a dozen solutions for this inconsistency if he'd thought about it longer than a minute. It's his responsibility to be at least *that* careful, if not much more. But he didn't. He wasn't. And it annoys me, when other flaws please and delight me.

Cut to three men piling out of a "police station" into a "police car." One of these men is Tor Johnson, instantly recognizable from his bulk. The car does a pretty sloppy job of leaving the station, and the maneuver reveals a small, harsh cone of lighting projected onto the dark sidewalk and street for the shot. The car speeds along a dirt road somewhere in Los Angeles in lighting that could generously be called day for night.[37] It pulls to a stop half out of frame in an absolutely terrible shot. The camera tries to pan left to catch the characters leaving the car but doesn't quite make it. Back to the studio cemetery, and Criswell's narration, for the police arrival. Tor is identified as Inspector Daniel Clay. They meet another policeman already on the scene (Larry) and pass some lines about the situation.

Tor Johnson's delivery is not great, but it's not worth unkindness. Besides, Wood's dialogue is, was, and always will be the most incomprehensible part of any of his scenes.

Tor walks through heavy mist. He takes out his gun. The music is apprehensive. Near the gravediggers' bodies, a policeman in a trenchcoat

[37] "Day for night" is when cinematographers adjust camera settings and/or editors adjust exposure techniques so that a scene filmed in daylight is dim enough to appear to be night. This phenomenon is visible everywhere in movies of all budgets and calibers across the 20th century, from *Attack of the Giant Leeches* to *Psycho*. It can occasionally be successful, in black and white, with the right conditions, but it usually isn't (and in color, it isn't even passable). Daylight looks like daylight, with sharp shadows and ambient illumination—especially in bright, sunny southern California, where so much 20th century American film was shot—whereas nighttime just doesn't look like that. With the technology available during the classical Hollywood period, it was expensive and difficult to film on location at night, and the footage often looked bad. The previous shot of this very film, when the three men leave the police station, indicates fairly well the limitations of night shooting.

(Lieutenant Harper) comments, "Looks like a bobcat tore into 'em." At the sound of a siren, he identifies it as the "morgue wagon."

Cut to the Trent patio, in the sole graceful bit of filmmaking in all 78 minutes of *Plan 9 from Outer Space*, where Paula Trent says, "That's the fifth siren in the last hour." This transition, unlike every other, draws a genuine connection between what we just saw and what we're seeing now. This patio must be close to the cemetery, or these characters would not have heard the same siren as the policemen. But they did, unmistakably. The sound bridge across the cut, plus comments by two characters on either side of the cut, told us so. This is good work by Wood, and I credit him for it.

An inept, unfortunate conversation follows between Jeff and Paula. Jeff reveals that he saw "a flying *saucer*" "shaped like a huge *cigar*," an inconsistency we might have been able to forgive because "flying saucer" was vernacular for UFOs at the time, but we saw it too, out the window of Jeff's cockpit, and it was not shaped like a cigar at all. Jeff explains that "big Army brass" swooped down on him after his plane landed and had him swear not to tell anyone about what he'd seen, which is of course why he's telling his wife.[38] He also seems irate that despite it being "a fact" that UFOs "have been seen for years," he can't tell anyone about it (again, aside from Paula).

The dialogue does something frustrating here: it doubles back on itself.

PAULA

There must be something more you can do about it.

JEFF

Only there isn't. Oh, but what's the use of making a fuss. But last night I saw a flying object that couldn't possibly have been from this planet. But I can't say a word! I'm muzzled by army brass!

---

[38] I stole this joke from the RiffTrax of *Plan 9 from Outer Space*.

Jeff's speech shows him waffling between convictions: *I can't do anything about this situation, and I see no point in speaking up, but I'm angry and I want to speak up*. It's reasonable that in real life a person might think and feel all this simultaneously, but in fiction, one "but" after another makes a character look foolish and indecisive.

Of course, indecisiveness *can* be displayed in fiction. It's not illegal. But it takes time and care to show a character genuinely struggling,[39] rather than making the character seem like kind of an idiot. In this scene, the screenwriter appears to be wasting our time, as Jeff cycles through one idea after another too rapidly to make us believe he's truly considering them.

A flying saucer passes overhead just then. Jeff and Paula fall down awkwardly. Cut to the cemetery, and two men carrying a stretcher. The policemen fall down, a corpse tumbles into some hay (??), and a falling ambulance attendant kicks a tombstone, which wobbles. Tor sees the saucer too, and so do we. It lands in the cemetery still photo again. Tor, gun drawn, passes the playhouse crypt, from which emerges a man with a Dracula cape drawn over his nose.

This man is definitely not Bela Lugosi, but it is so plainly meant to be Lugosi that I won't waste many more words on it. Somehow this flaw is less egregious to me than Vampira being set up as Lugosi's wife. Actors die; recasting happens. Wood's solution, to cast a man who doesn't resemble Lugosi in *any* way except hairline, and to have that man just cover most of his face every time he's on camera, is pretty stupid. But it's far from the stupidest thing in the film.

The music intensifies as Tor wanders around the set, until, oh no! Vampira appears. She and faux-Lugosi tag-team Tor (in separate shots), with offscreen results. The useful information in this sequence is that the ghouls are not affected by bullets.

The policemen hear Tor's gunshots and find him dead. Lt. Harper says very dumb dialogue ("Inspector Clay's dead—murdered—and *somebody's* responsible"), and gestures with his gun as if it's a mere prop rather than a deadly weapon.

Cut to funeral no. 3 within 20 minutes. The editing suggests that Vampira is one of Clay's mourners.

---

[39] Cf *Hamlet*, a very long play.

Cut to flying saucers (3), and so begins a baffling montage. Criswell narrates, mostly in the style of a newsreel.

1) Footage of the 101 freeway in Hollywood: from the highway looking south, and then of a car with people pointing out of it.
2) A printing press runs.
3) Man unfolds newspaper: SAUCERS SEEN OVER HOLLYWOOD.
4) CBS building with badly processed saucer overlay effect.
5) Lady looking out of phone booth.
6) NBC building with saucer overlay.
7) Phone booth lady again, making a call. Criswell tries to connect this footage to the flying saucers.
8) Newspaper near coffee paraphernalia, same headline as no. 3.
9) Saucer over darker sky than before.
10) Drunken-stumbling man picks up newspaper near garbage can, same headline as nos. 3 and 8.
11) Probable Hollywood street at night (lots of neon) with saucer overlay. Two shots.
12) Guy outside bar in daytime looks up, rubs eyes, glances at booze bottle in hand. Back to night shot as in no. 11; back to man, who puts bottle down.
13) UFOs against outer space-type sky-with-stars backdrop. They appear drunk as well.
14) Passenger plane above Pentagon, Washington Monument in background.
15) Some kind of spinning radar dish. Saucer. Dish.
16) Military jeeps filled with helmeted men drive down a dirt road. Saucer (visible shadow on backdrop). Jeep with missiles, clearly in the desert, nowhere near Washington (or Hollywood, for that matter). Saucers.
17) Men loading large missiles into something. Houses in background. Man looks into eyepiece of some kind of large weapon.

18) Colonel Edwards, in front of the blankest backdrop in the film, lifts binoculars to his eyes.

From here, we move into a second, more explicitly military montage, which alternates between no. 18, shots of the saucers, and various military footage.

The first montage lasts about two minutes. If I squint, I can see what Wood was trying to do: demonstrate that the saucers are a national issue, not one local to the cemetery near the Trents' house; and transition between the UFOs in Hollywood[40] (the previous bit of the film) to the military operation of which Col. Edwards is a part (the next bit of the film).

It's hard to imagine how, on his budget, Wood could perform these moves more directly, rather than using the indirect methods of Criswell's voiceover and the assembled stock footage. That sentence is me being fair to Wood's external limitations. But the solution of this montage is no solution at all. It introduces a bunch of new settings and faces we'll never see again, and inserts footage we absolutely do not need (no. 2, no. 12, no. 16). It's possible that Wood thought the audience would believe *he* had shot the footage of Hollywood—the CBS and NBC buildings, for instance—and be impressed. But that is beside the point, which is that no audience can follow and squeeze meaning from a sequence of two dozen shots that barely connect to each other and have hardly anything to do with what came before.

And this brings us back to the single biggest problem with *Plan 9 from Outer Space*: its networked-but-disconnected jumble of ideas, the failure of its plot summary to convey a sense of what happens on screen. (See p. 9). A good montage should connect with some or all of what came before it and prepare us for the next sequence of the film.[41] I can see Wood straining toward this goal, but he completely misses it. The montage

---

[40] The movie implies somewhat successfully that the Trents live in or near Hollywood. Jeff's copilot reports to Burbank Tower on his radio, and refers to "the old San Fernando Valley" as a visible landmark in his first line. Also, the still photograph of the cemetery has palm trees in it. A later scene more directly indicates that the Trents live in San Fernando, but at this point in the movie it's all implication.

[41] Cf, for instance, every athletic training montage in every 1980s movie. They reflect back on the character's journey to this point and prepare him, and us, for what he will have to do next. Their main purpose is to show time passing and/or a slow change occurring in a compressed amount of screen time, but it's key that they connect to scenes and elements before and after.

connects to earlier scenes only by virtue of the UFOs (no Lugosi, no Vampira; other characters *see* the saucers, but the significance of this seeing has yet to be revealed). It prepares us for the sequences involving Col. Edwards, in a way, but the military footage (nos. 16 and 17) is, of all the shots in the montage, most plainly stock footage. Col. Edwards standing in front of nothing at all immediately follows rough, well-used shots of men in front of a landscape with actual houses on it, which makes clear the distinction between what was filmed by Wood and what was not.

So little that happens in this montage connects to what comes before and after, and so little of it matters to the film as a whole. I can summarize the purpose of the montage (as above), but that summary does not include the lady in the phone booth or the two drunks, because those characters add no significance to the summary, or, consequently, to the film as a whole. They may as well not be in the film for all they add to it. Similarly, the two scenes to come with Col. Edwards before he travels to Hollywood have almost no significance to the plot of *Plan 9* as summarized (aliens reanimate the dead in order to get Earthlings to understand the threat they pose to the universe). He's present at the confrontation that closes the film, and he's relevant to the supposed national issue of the saucers, but his screen time is disproportionate to his importance to the main plot of the film. He does not drive the plot nor contribute to it; he's just…nearby. And he gets a lot of scenes for someone who's just nearby.

Wood has a hard time sticking to the plot, as this montage shows. It demonstrates the problems with *Plan 9* in miniature: trying to use editing to solve problems editing cannot solve, cheap/inadequate props and sets and visual strategies, filler that makes viewers lose the thread.

Confusion of the kind in this montage halts us in our tracks and keeps us from going with the flow of the movie. We notice all of a sudden that we're watching a movie, one that isn't making any sense to us, instead of living a little bit inside the movie. Further, because we're trying to figure out what's going on, we tend not to remember what we're seeing. Little of what we see sticks in our minds until the movie starts to make sense again. It's a major problem with confusing movies (those not confusing because of deliberate artistic intent, that is): the way our memories erase what doesn't make sense until almost the whole movie vanishes.

On into the second montage. Criswell's voiceover identifies Edwards as "Colonel Tom Edwards in charge of saucer field activities." I do not have an adequate quip for that job description, especially considering that its existence renders two later scenes totally inconsistent. Col. Edwards "fires" on the saucers, which leads to a series of interspersed shots: stock footage of military men firing large-caliber missile-type weapons, bottle rockets popping near saucers dangling before the cloudy-sky backdrop, and Col. Edwards in his solitary void. He lifts his binoculars and lowers them a few times. The music suggests something very exciting is happening.

The film stock of the military footage is so distinct from the stock of the saucer/Edwards footage that they don't even cut together especially well, forming a jarring sequence that fails to communicate an intention passing from Col. Edwards to the missiles to the saucers. Also, the tiny explosions by the saucers try to communicate scale, but they don't, because the saucers are so clearly props.

This montage hangs together a little better than the one preceding it, but exactly because of that montage's confusion, this Edwards-related sequence doesn't really sink in or matter to the audience. We stopped trying to parse this movie during the prior two minutes. Edwards seems as much like a character we need to remember as the lady in the telephone booth.

Which is why it's a bit surprising when a helmeted Army captain with a giant walkie-talkie joins Col. Edwards in his void, and then speaks dialogue to him. We've heard only Criswell for a few chaotic minutes, and here we are in an actual scene!

It's a pretty poor scene, one which contradicts itself almost surreally (see pp. 18–20 for a full explanation), and it includes this line:

EDWARDS

For a time we tried to contact them by radio, but no response. Then they attacked a town. A small town, I'll admit. But nevertheless a town of people. People who died.

This line, *so* badly written, produces nothing but questions. Is he talking about where the Trents live? If so, who died in the Trents' town? Why didn't we see a scene of that happening? Or hear any reference to it until now? If it's another town, which town? And why haven't we heard any reference to *that*? Is this movie meant to be a record of all UFO contact with Earth? If so, why leave this fatal conflict out? Or is it a record of some other sequence of events? By what logic does this movie portray them?

Edwards asks a few questions of his own, the captain offers up his nonsensical, contradictory last line, and then, to finish the scene, Edwards says "I wonder what their next move will be."

Cut to "space," where tiny saucers hover around a mother ship roughly shaped like the planet Saturn[42] and crowned with a nipple.

CRISWELL

What will their next move be?

Dissolve to a curtained set containing two desks with a bunch of

[42] To me, it most closely resembles an 1980s toy called a Pogo Ball. But you, reader, are likely more familiar with Saturn.

sciencey equipment piled on top. For once, this shot makes sense. Criswell's voiceover plus the space shot have served as setup, establishing that the men in this room are aliens and we're about to learn what their next move will be. But it took a twice-repeated line and a longish establishing shot to set that down. The sciencey equipment helps, along with the costume of the man who enters through the curtains. He wears leggings and a satin tunic, adorned with a lightning bolt on the left breast, with a gun at his waist. It signals "uniform," and, if you've watched enough 1950s sci-fi flicks, "alien."

The man at the desk does not get a name. The other characters call him "Excellency," the credits call him "Leader," and the script calls him "Ruler." For simplicity's sake I will call him Bunny, which was the nickname of the actor.

Soon, Eros and Tanna enter in the same uniforms. The scene that follows is largely expository, and not terrible on its face, except that the ideas presented are so laughable. Here we learn the meaning of "Plan 9"—it is the strategy (such as it is) the aliens have chosen to implement on Earth.[43]

Eros tells Bunny that they have already begun to implement Plan 9, which "deals with the resurrection of the dead," by "rising" two of the "recent dead." If the audience can remember back before the montage, we will be able to connect what Eros says to the gradual menace of Vampira and faux-Lugosi. Big if. Eros explains that they had to kill a policeman (Tor), but that the Earthlings suspect nothing. What they *could* suspect, based on what has occurred, is unclear.

Tanna gets a medium shot, but no dialogue until they leave Bunny's room.[44] Outside, she and Eros chat a bit, to reinforce the scene we've just watched, and attempt to speculate about what's coming next.

TANNA

```
What do you think will be the next obstacle
   the Earth people will put in our way?
```

---

[43] I enjoy the idea of a little file cabinet full of plans from which the aliens make a choice every time they find a new planet.

[44] Though "Bunny's room" is a strange thing to call a set, I cannot see my way to calling it an office.

EROS

Well, as long as they can think, we'll have our problems. But those whom we're using cannot think. They are the dead. Brought to a simulated life by our electrode guns. You know, it's an interesting thing when you consider...the Earth people, who can think, are so frightened by those who cannot: the dead.

If this scene were any good, Eros would answer Tanna's question so as to set up the next morsel of the plot. That is what good scenes do: they are individual vertebrae, providing continuity and structure to the whole. Tanna's question is a good start to a decent scene, because—like Criswell's "What will their next move be?"—it's a question that the audience may also be asking, and the film can answer. But Eros does not answer her question at all. He reveals common knowledge (the dead cannot think) and ruminates shallowly on something that doesn't bear on the plot.

Asking and answering too baldly in a screenplay is no good, either, as the movie begins to feel like a puppet show. But in this instance, either Tanna should not have asked this question, or Eros should have answered it, if the scene was meant to convey any kind of audience satisfaction. Eros's answer connects to hardly anything of substance we've already seen or will see. Without reaching backward and looking forward, scenes are just filler.

Filler scenes waste the audience's time on "shoe-leather," a term which unfortunately means two totally disparate things in creative writing. In journalism, it means an old-fashioned, active method of information-gathering: going to multiple places and talking to sources rather than sitting glued to a computer. In other forms of creative writing, it means expending space and time on moves that can easily be inferred rather than described. If, in a short story, an author describes a man getting up from the couch and going to the door to answer a ringing doorbell, the man has used up some of his shoe-leather walking from one place to another, and the author has wasted the words to describe it when she could have jumped to the important part. "The doorbell rang. Sheryl stood on the doorstep," is better than "The doorbell rang. He stood up from the couch, walked across the room, and answered the door. Sheryl stood on the doorstep." That middle sentence purports to offer information about how a character gets from point A to point B, but such detail about a journey from the couch to the door is almost always unnecessary.

In movies, shoe-leather scenes come in several varieties. Bad movies generally have many more scenes of cars driving and parking than good movies.[45] Brainless filmmakers include these scenes because they presume the audience will not comprehend how a character traveled from home to office without a driving-and-parking scene to explain it. (We will.) Filmmakers with woes related to running time include these scenes to pad a thin film to feature length. In another variation on shoe-leather, characters might do chores or have domestic conversations that have no bearing on the plot and are too mundane to genuinely build character. In *Silent Rage* (1982), a character who appears and then dies within ten minutes of screen time learns across a page or two of dialogue that her homemade cinnamon cake is bad; in *Deadly Prey* (1987), the main character and his wife banter about him getting up late in the morning. In any manifestation, shoe-leather scenes are a sign that a filmmaker has minimal respect for his audience.

This scene with Eros and Tanna outside Bunny's room isn't a shoe-leather scene, but a scene that wandered away from its purpose at some point during drafting and was never reexamined to give it focus. That's why Eros's final lines *feel* like shoe-leather. If Eros had given Tanna an answer, we would know where we were going, narratively, and the movie would imply it has some confidence. But he doesn't, because there is no answer to her question. No obstacles against Plan 9 ever materialize. The rest of the movie involves the human characters confronting the plan's outcome (the ghouls) and then... Eros talking to them. That's it. There is no conflict, or at least not a conflict with organic stakes and consequences like the one Tanna's question posits.

In this one scene, this one line of Tanna's, not even halfway through, the

---

[45] I owe a debt of gratitude to the writers at RiffTrax for this insight, which they note in *many* movies.

film collapses—shows itself as a jumble of half-baked ideas rather than a story. If Eros had an answer, the movie would have something like a plot. But he doesn't, and it doesn't.

EROS

```
Well, our ship should be regenerated. We
better get started.
```

Off the saucers go. They leave the mother ship and hover in a darkened cloud-backdrop shot. Cut to the Trent patio, Paula with a magazine and Jeff leaving the house dressed in his pilot's uniform. They have a vacuous con-versation, sort of about Paula's safety in light of the flying saucers and the weird events at the cemetery, which evidently still register as two separate threats. She goes inside and Jeff leaves, getting into a convertible (on the passenger side) parked against a black backdrop as stark as Col. Edwards's void.

Dissolve to an establishing shot of a passenger plane in flight. Cut to the cockpit set. The scene that follows accomplishes very little, aside from straight-facedly using the phrase "balling it up in Albuquerque." Jeff worries over Paula's safety. Edie the flight attendant performs some wordplay that isn't really a joke and then apologizes: "I'm sorry, Jeff, that was a bad joke." Also, she encourages Jeff to use the plane's radio to request a check-in on Paula.

Lightning crashes, somewhere. Cut to Bela Lugosi, the real one, in full Dracula costume, tramping through the location cemetery from the first funeral scene. Criswell identifies him as "THE DEAD OLD MAN!" He spreads his cape wide and walks off. Dissolve to Lugosi almost entering the side door of a house, a rapid shot which offers us no useful information, as we have not seen this side door before. Cut to a fairly well-composed high-angle shot of Paula, asleep in bed with an open book near her elbow. The telephone rings. She rouses and answers it. She speaks to "Mac," who is, multiple viewings have helped me to understand, the radio operator at Burbank Tower. Although the previous scene set up that Jeff was going to radio in and ask for a call like this, "Mac" is not well-established as the radio operator's name, vs. a nickname like "bud" or "buster." Plus, the chain of plausibility has weak links along the way: that Paula would know Mac's name, that Mac would have nothing better to do (as an *air traffic controller*) than call Paula to check on her.[46]

Quick cut to Lugosi entering the side door, then back to Paula's bedroom for a wider shot. The bedroom door opens, and in comes faux-Lugosi, covering his face so aggressively that I doubt the actor could see where he was going. Paula screams and runs, and he pursues her at a gentle mosey. She runs through the studio cemetery, a white flash in the darkness; cut to real Lugosi leaving the side door.

This series of shots communicates adequately, if not perfectly, that the man in the bedroom is supposed to be Bela Lugosi, THE DEAD OLD MAN. For once, the editing explains across the obvious continuity problem of faux-Lugosi, rather than just confusing us. It is still laughable that the two men are meant to be one, but the mechanics of what Wood means to communicate are, on this occasion, not too sloppy. We do have to connect the side door Lugosi enters with Paula's bedroom, but since the side door is a night shot, it's possible. It would have been better to see Paula entering or exiting the same side door at some point.

Paula runs through an indistinct landscape and trips. Vampira peers through some dead branches. Cut back to Paula, in a fully lit shot, getting to her feet in the studio cemetery. She runs left. Cut to real Lugosi walking into the location cemetery again. Shot of a grave headed by a tiny gravestone, the shape of a pencil eraser. The soil over the grave moves and shifts as if something's underneath it. This shot would be creepy if it weren't surrounded by so much incompetence.

Vampira walks away from the camera, evidently through crunchy dead leaves. She half-turns and gives something out of frame an assessing look, then continues. Faux-Lugosi moves through the studio cemetery. In a lightning-fast shot, Paula runs through the same portion of the cemetery she's already run through. Grave soil moves in a much lengthier shot. Paula runs from a different angle, away from the camera. Grave soil tumbles into the grave, a very nice effect. Vampira walks, arms out in zombie stance, right to left across the frame. Grave soil collapses completely. Paula runs (well, jogs), screaming.

---

[46] A line cut from the screenplay indicates that Mac "thrives on doing favors for the pilots." Still.

Then, a wonderful shot: Tor Johnson rises out of a grave, lit from beneath, eyes blank, shadow looming. It's great, except he only gets a third of the way up before he begins to struggle and rock against the side of the grave. He wiggles like a fish. It's unfortunate. (Also, the stone behind him doesn't match the pencil-eraser gravestone, so it doesn't really follow that the grave with the collapsing soil is the same one he's coming out of.) Cut to a different angle of Tor, in a different position, standing up. The two shots and actions do not match at all, and the cut and blocking drain some of the menace from the initial creepy shot of Tor.

Paula runs. Now that Tor's out of the ground, each of the ghouls gets their own shot, but the shot length isn't quite parallel. The rhythm is choppy and fails to ratchet up the tension. None of the ghouls looks that fearsome, perhaps because we haven't seen them do anything too scary. Between Tor and Vampira, a shot of the pencil-eraser gravestone falling into the pile of loose dirt. Although what occurs in that shot will be important later, right now it doesn't connect to Tor. There is no visually consistent indication that he rose from *that* soil, rather than a second location with a larger gravestone. The landmarks don't match.

Paula runs again, downstage to upstage. Tor moves left to right. Faux-

Lugosi stalks downstage to upstage. The breeze from his cape sets a-wobble a grave marker shaped like a cross.

Then, suddenly, we're on location, in day-for-night, and a car drives into frame on the right. On the left, a woman in a diaphanous nightgown like Paula's emerges from the grass at the side of the road and runs along the shoulder. I cannot emphasize enough how bad the framing is here. The idea, I think, is for the car to encounter Paula as she runs out of the cemetery and takes a comical nosedive at the side of the road. But the camera keeps panning with tentative, halting motions, trying to get the movements of both subjects in the same frame as they both move left. The effect is amateurish.

A shot of the driver (Farmer),[47] a husky guy in a white cowboy hat, is interrupted by a shot of faux-Lugosi, I believe to indicate that these two characters are in approximately the same location in spacetime, but the lighting and locations are completely different and it doesn't come off. Shots alternate between the ghouls and Farmer, who knows Paula.

FARMER

`Mrs. Trent! Mrs. Trent! What's wrong?`

She seems to have fainted. Farmer picks her up and carries her into his car. The editing suggests that the three ghouls (actually four—there's a shot of real Lugosi in there) are closing in on Farmer and Paula, despite all other evidence that they are nowhere nearby. After the car drives off, faux-Lugosi walks patiently after it, then breaks off, back to the field that the editing has indicated is the cemetery, based on where Paula came running into the road. Vampira and Tor also walk . . . away, although there is no kind of implied "to" or "from" in the geography of this sequence. They are each in their own shots, and they each turn and go the other way from where they were going, and that is all.

Where to begin. This is meant to be one of the scary sequences of *Plan 9*, this attack on Paula by the ghouls, but it is almost entirely unscary. Part

---

[47] He's called "Farmer" in the credits, but I have no idea what's supposed to communicate that. He's driving a convertible. Still, it's the name Wood gave him, so I'll use it.

of the reason is the movie's general shoddiness, but there's also a mild failure of stakes and a geography problem.

Although the film has told us that the two gravediggers were torn apart, as if a bobcat had been at them, we have likely forgotten that, with all we've been through since then. It's not immediately clear, in this sequence, what will happen to Paula if the ghouls catch her. What kind of danger is she in? We know via dialogue only, not visuals. Also, we can't believe the danger is that exigent, since we only see Paula in the same shot as any of the ghouls a few times, and they walk in no particular hurry as she runs. Are they really so close on her heels?[48]

Further, the editing implies—not terribly, but not well—that all these characters are in near proximity. But we simply cannot know where they are in relation to each other without a) two-shots,[49] where the distance between two characters is evident, or b) landmarks, where two characters move past the same object or structure so we know approximately where they each are. In so many of the shots in this sequence—almost all of them—a character stands in or moves through his or her surroundings totally alone, and those surroundings do not have landmarks that match those in the other characters' solo shots. That is, Paula runs through a field with no identifying landmarks, so when faux-Lugosi walks through a field with no identifying landmarks, how do we know it's the same field? Vampira stands near some dead tree branches, and Tor walks by some, too, but they are so indistinguishable that it would take an overlay to tell if they're in the same place.

When a landscape is indistinct, and characters have too many separate shots, the audience cannot connect the movements of individual characters to each other. (Remember those three Ls.) A distinct landscape helps us draw a rudimentary map of the action in our minds and comprehend the danger our characters are in. *Alien* (1979) illustrates this concept in the computer tracking scene, where Ripley watches the alien dot and the Dallas dot move closer to each other, until one dot blinks no more. Most action scenes don't literally map out like this, but they do

---

[48] This is common enough to be a horror trope—the shambling monster and the sprinting victim. But it hardly helps.

[49] Moviemaking term for "shot with two people in it."

usually offer visual landmarks to help us understand how the characters are moving through space and how close they are to each other.

A related problem is when limited sets lead to contradictory geography. Paula runs through the same shot of the studio cemetery in two different directions: first toward the camera, and then away. Then, Faux-Lugosi, supposedly pursuing her, walks through the set away from the camera. He's following her most recent move, but with the chaotic editing and repeated solo shots, there's no way the audience can be sure of that. The set is so small that there's no sense of pursuit, just of two characters going in circles. The film tries to use right-to-left and left-to-right blocking tricks to indicate that the characters are moving through the same landscape, or that one is pursuing the other, but Wood doesn't have the attention to detail and consistency required to make maneuvers like this work.

After the action scene is over (we can tell because the theme music ends), a police car wails along the same road Farmer drove along to find Paula, and possibly the same road the police car came along to get to the cemetery earlier in the film. It drives right to left, implying that it's following Farmer's car. But then we cut to the police car pulling up at the studio cemetery, from which Farmer drove *away*. I could excuse this in isolation by saying, well, it's all in the same neighborhood, whatever. But the truth is that Wood doesn't know how to block a series of scenes, or possibly doesn't know that such blocking is required for a movie to make spatial sense. This is just the latest example of it.

Four policemen get out of the car. One last shot of real Lugosi in the location cemetery, and then he flings his cape around his shoulder in a practiced gesture and heads offscreen. We'll see him once more, but this is the exit I prefer to remember as his last.

The policemen wander through the cemetery, looking for something, although what it could be we do not know. How the police knew to come to the cemetery when Paula was in danger (if their arrival is even related to her) is also a mystery; we don't see evidence that anyone called the police, and too little time seems to have passed between Farmer driving away with her and the police arriving.

At last, Vampira and Tor appear in the same shot, and as monsters go, they rank as "strong attempts at scary." If we could have taken any of the film seriously up to now, they might look scarier. They walk from left to right.

Cut to a new set: the inside of Eros's ship. He and Tanna gaze out the window, to the left of frame. This, that the ghouls walk right and the aliens look left, plus the music overlap, plus Eros's next line, "They'll be at the hatch in a moment," combine to form a good indication that Eros and Tanna are looking at Vampira and Tor. Yet there is still no *geographical* indication that these two shots occur in physical proximity. (Plus, we brought in the police for a second only to drop them.)

Finally, here *Plan 9* connects Vampira and Tor with the aliens. The film has not succeeded in doing this so far, despite trying.[50] The scene in Bunny's room doesn't even really manage it; we can understand the plan, but the ghouls (especially Vampira) are so blank, so hard to read, that it's far easier to consider them motivation-free monsters without a past or future than elements of the plan the aliens discussed. Plus, the connections between the aliens and the cemetery where the ghouls stalk are weakly made. We can't immediately believe that the cemetery photograph in which the saucer lands is the same place as the studio cemetery, nor that the toy saucer which lands in that photo is the same place as the room in which Eros and Tanna now stand. It takes a lot of leaps to get where Wood wants us to go, and we are short on springboards.

These connections could have been made, or made stronger, in a variety of ways. Showing Eros and Tanna leaving the saucer in the studio cemetery earlier on in the running time might have done it. Or a line in the scene with Bunny about Eros's landing location. Or a shot of Vampira or Tor in the same frame as the saucer. Or some kind of recurrent musical motif. Or a conversation between some of the other characters about seeing something specific in the cemetery, rather than just lights and sounds. Naming the cemetery, to show that all the various landscapes are meant to be the same location, would have helped. There are many solutions to the jagged continuity of location and event in this movie, and Wood implemented none of them.

[50] Multiple viewings have made me suspect that Wood wanted us to make this connection much earlier in the film, maybe as early as the gravediggers' death. But he also purposely writes the characters *not* making the connection. Sophisticated stories can allow the audience to know more than the characters, but this is just chaos.

Vampira and Tor enter the ship. Tanna demonstrates that the aliens have physical control over the ghouls. Cut to faux-Lugosi, approaching a structure that is meant to be the outside of Eros's ship. We can tell because the door that opens for him makes the same sound and motion as the one that opened inside the ship for Vampira and Tor. (*That's* continuity that grounds us with a landmark. See how easy it is?) Visually, the structure faux-Lugosi enters bears no resemblance to the round, silvery saucer we've seen so frequently. This isn't an easy problem to solve without money, but building a structure with squared-off sides and a ladder, and claiming it's a disc-shaped UFO, is a poor effort.

Behind Eros and Tanna are two windows, one a black square and the other a daytime cloudscape. Since the two windows are *right next to each other*, and thus should be showing approximately the same view, this mistake is particularly silly. It exists in all the scenes that occur in this room.

Two cops enter the studio cemetery and exchange bad dialogue.

POLICEMAN

It's tough to find something when you don't know what you're looking for.

Comforting to know he's as confused as we are.

The saucer takes off from the cemetery photo. Lt. Harper and Larry hear it but don't seem to see it.

LARRY

What do you suppose that noise was?

LT. HARPER

Whatever it was, it's no more strange than the other things happening around this cemetery.

There's a bad, bad cut in this scene, simply switching from one angle on a two-shot of Lt. Harper and Larry to another angle on the same pair. It's the kind of cut that low-quality filmmakers use to conceal poor or incomplete takes, and it's disorienting, like blinking and finding you've magically switched seats in your living room.

Larry affirms that they've come to the cemetery based on a report from Farmer and Paula, although based on the editing, the timing doesn't really work. If Wood had *dissolved* from the ghouls moving away (individually) through the cemetery to the police car pulling up, it would have indicated the passage of time. But he simply *cut*, which makes it seem like the two events happened in immediate sequence. Which is illogical.

The other two cops come rushing up, and the four of them talk about the noise of the saucer taking off. Lt. Harper seems confident that the noise is/was a saucer, when not even 60 seconds ago he wouldn't speculate ("Whatever it was . . .").

The writing in this scene demonstrates that, at least when he wrote it, Wood wanted to keep balancing the characters' apprehension of strange goings-on in the cemetery between the ghouls and the flying saucers, without the characters understanding that the two phenomena are related. The way the characters assess the threat in the film swings between these two phenomena almost at random. The police seek answers for first one phenomenon, and then the other. Lt. Harper and Larry, on their own, talked about the ghouls, while the foursome talks about saucers. There's no consistency across the two conversations.

Here's the scene between the four cops in full.

```
                    KELTON
   Lieutenant, Lieutenant! Did you hear that?

                    LARRY
           How could we help it?

                  POLICEMAN
            It sure was strange.

                    KELTON
             Know what it was?
```

LARRY
No more than you do.

POLICEMAN
If it weren't for orders I'd get out of here right now.

LT. HARPER
It was a saucer.

POLICEMAN
A flying saucer?

LARRY
What makes you say that?

LT. HARPER
You remember the noise we heard the other night?

LARRY
We were knocked to the ground! How could I forget?

LT. HARPER
Exactly, but you're not remembering that sound.

LARRY
There you're wrong, Lieutenant. I'm with the fact the sound is similar, but what about the blinding light?

LT. HARPER
Well, haven't you heard? Many times a saucer

hasn't had a glow, or a light of any kind, for that matter.

LARRY

That proves it. What next, Lieutenant?

The inconsistency and stiltedness of this dialogue speaks for itself. Each line rushes into the last uncomfortably (especially "Exactly" and "That proves it"). I don't even know what to say about "Haven't you heard?" Sometimes analysis fails me.

In the screenplay, this scene and its purpose are clearer. Sometimes the saucer that lands in the cemetery makes both sound and light, and sometimes it does not. This scene tries to point out that it can still be a saucer whether it makes both sound and light or not, and tries to get these policemen to all agree that they heard and saw a saucer the other night and, this evening, have heard it but not seen it, *and yet* it was probably the same saucer. Believe me that the screenplay does not make it *much* clearer, and that Wood should have implemented better, more consistent special effects and done at least one rewrite if he really wanted to get this across.

The conversation turns back to the ghouls—again, the ghouls and the saucers have been patched together here and there across the screenplay, rather than interwoven. Kelton and Unnamed Cop[51] have discovered a grave with freshly upturned dirt. Lt. Harper puts his foot up on the side of the grave, but we don't see what the cops are seeing. The grave is just offscreen. That means we can't compare it to either the grave from the moving-soil shots (with the pencil-eraser gravestone) or the grave from the Tor-gets-stuck shots. No wide shots encompass the disturbed grave or Kelton going into it. We just see medium shots of the policemen. This is not helpful in connecting the location of their conversation to where Tor rose from the dead.

The policemen expend some dialogue about the disturbed grave, including one of the two major self-contradictions in the film.

---

[51] I think his name is Jamie, but I wouldn't put money on it. The script doesn't specify.

LARRY

Do we have the right to look down there, Lieutenant?

LT. HARPER

Ah, technically, no.

LARRY

No?

LT. HARPER

Well, this spot looks familiar, though. We shouldn't investigate any further without the permission of next of kin.

KELTON

Let's go get it!

LT. HARPER

How?

LARRY

I see what you mean. The gravestone's down there.

LT. HARPER

Well, let's go down and find out whose grave it is.

KELTON

How?

LT. HARPER

By going down and finding out!

The dialogue intends to say:

1. The policemen don't have permission to "look down" into the grave without the permission of next of kin.

2. The policemen can't find out who the next of kin are without looking at the gravestone to figure out to whom the grave belongs.

3. The gravestone is inside the grave.

4. Thus, in order to find out whether they have permission to go into the grave, they must go into the grave.

Let's break this down.

1. Generally, in America, burial lots are owned by cemeteries and sold for burials under easement.[52] That means the people buried there and their loved ones don't own the land or the soil—the cemetery does. So next of kin doesn't enter into it, except as a courtesy. The laws about disturbing graves seem to vary widely, and depend on context (whether the disturbance was for some practical reason, or for desecration or robbery). But stepping into a disturbed grave for what I guess are informational purposes does not appear to be a civil or criminal offense.[53] If it was, permission would come from the cemetery, or potentially from the police, which . . . these men are.[54]

2. Looking at the gravestone is not the only way to figure out to whom the grave belongs. Cemeteries keep records of such things. Also, these men were *just here*, likely less than a week ago, for Inspector Clay's funeral. How can they not remember that this is where he's buried?

3. The pencil-eraser gravestone fell into the grave, but it's insufficiently clear that the pencil-eraser gravestone belonged to Clay's grave. So this item, too, is disputable.

4. This is a paradox. Lt. Harper is visibly annoyed when he says "By

[52] "In nearly all jurisdictions, one who purchases and has conveyed to him/her a lot in a public cemetery does not acquire the fee to the soil." https://www.stimmel-law.com/en/articles/basic-laws-pertaining-cemeteries

[53] At least, not according to Dr. Google.

[54] The screenplay includes this line from Lt. Harper: "We'll waive regulations this time," after "By going down there and finding out." So it's not as contradictory as the finished film. But that one line does not save the scene. And if it could have, Wood should damn well have shot it.

going down and finding out!" as if Kelton should have known exactly what he meant, despite him saying, literal seconds ago, that they cannot go into the grave.

In sum: none of the premises of the scene hold up.

I cannot believe that actors with working brains, moving through this scene, wouldn't ask aloud, *hey, why doesn't this scene make any sense?* I cannot believe that Wood could write and film this scene and not realize how contradictory it is. Everything about these lines of dialogue is inexcusably daft.

Kelton goes into the grave. He asks for a flashlight or a match to read the name on the casket,[55] in a bit of shoe-leather that is a waste of screen time and editing, because he easily could have brought a match or a flashlight into the grave with him and absolutely nothing is gained from him having to ask for one. He then proclaims, looking directly at the wall of soil in the side of the grave, "It's Inspector Clay's grave! But he ain't in it!"

Dissolve to a passenger plane over the Pentagon, which Criswell narrates:

```
                    CRISWELL
But meanwhile, in the Pentagon, in Washington, DC...
```

That's triplicate specificity: the visible landmark, the naming of it, and confirmation of the unobscure fact that the Pentagon is in DC. If only this kind of overdetermined clarity existed in the editing and blocking of the rest of the film.

The scene that follows is long by the standards of *Plan 9*, about five minutes. It involves Col. Edwards and his superior, General Roberts, talking at length about the phenomenon of flying saucers from the military point of view. The sequence is loaded with the kind of self-contradiction we previously saw in the scene with Col. Edwards and the captain. Both

---

[55] Are names commonly carved into caskets? I truly don't know the answer to this, particularly a 1956 answer, but it seems a bizarre assumption.[a] Also, how could he read the casket when a gravestone has collapsed into it? It seems most likely that the inside of that grave would just be a mess of dirt and a broken casket and a heavy-ass slab of stone, and nothing would be readable.[b]

[a] In the script, Harper asks if Kelton can read the name on the headstone. The word "casket" doesn't appear. So it's one of the actors' assumptions, I guess.

[b] These questions are in a footnote because I've spent too much time on this scene in the main text already. It's so much worse a scene than I thought it was.

these scenes have the same problem: Wood had to write a scene about UFOs and military men, yet had to maintain that the military denies knowledge of UFOs. He cannot write well enough to overcome this paradox, so the scenes are circular and nonsensical.[56]

This sequence bears many delights. Apropos of nothing, Gen. Roberts quietly says "I, uh, like you, Colonel," and speaks the phrase "atmospheric conditions in outer space," which makes sense if you do not expend a single neuron considering it.[57] The scene includes an audio recording of Eros, snarking at the human race for our inferiority and referring to our new invention, the "dictial robetary"[58] (the "language computer" or, as it's come to be known generally in sci-fi, the universal translator).

Overall, Eros's message isn't that different from Klaatu's speech at the end of *The Day the Earth Stood Still*: humans are irresponsible, and we build weapons way too dangerous for our own good and the good of the universe.[59] Klaatu's message includes a fascist solution, but Eros's offers no solution at all. Eros claims that "we don't want to conquer your planet, only to save it," which does not jibe with his hostile tone. He threatens with one phrase while offering friendship in the next.

The general says there have been a dozen transmissions like the one we just heard. It's unclear whether they all said the same thing or all bore different messages. That this could be the most substantive message of the dozen is unthinkable, as the recording tells us almost nothing about the aliens' planned actions or priorities. Nor does it articulate ideas that would be sensible for an interplanetary message: a request for a meeting, an explanation of whence it came, a suggestion of what kind of body it represents (a galactic alliance? a planetery army? a town council?). Also, this last transmission of 12 was received a month ago, which means the military has been remarkably slow to act upon this unprecedented, critically important situation.

Gen. Roberts sends Col. Edwards to Los Angeles—specifically, to San Fernando, where we can now presume the Trents live—to make contact

[56] This scene is exactly as contradictory in the screenplay as in the film.

[57] In the script, it's "Storms in outer space."

[58] This is the script's spelling. Craig, in *Ed Wood, Mad Genius*, posits that it's a mix-up of "robot dictionary," which I find cute as heck if true.

[59] This idea is at least as old as World War I, but still potent as I type this sentence.

with the UFOs and find out what they want, something their messages might logically have indicated.

We dissolve to the benippled mother ship, and then to Bunny's room. Eros reports on their progress to Bunny,[60] demonstrating the fruits of Plan 9 by presenting Tor, who sort of malfunctions and sort of tries to attack Eros. Breathlessly, Eros spits "That was . . . too close!" It was not. It was not even close.

The aliens discuss the next step: Eros must sacrifice faux-Lugosi to frighten the Earth people. Bunny finishes off with a series of ungrammatical sentences outlining the ultimate plan: "March [the ghouls] on the capitals of the Earth, let nothing stand in your way. Their own dead will be used to make them accept our existence, and believe in that fact."[61]

Based on this dialogue, the goal seems to be to get Earthlings to acknowledge the aliens, and listen to them, not for the aliens to conquer Earth. Even as I was drafting this monograph, I had a hard time understanding that, and kept writing sentences including the phrase "conquer Earth" without thinking about it. It's a major trope of science fiction films, from the 1950s forward, that aliens land on Earth in order to conquer it. These aliens' aggressiveness—in Eros's recorded message, in the details of Plan 9, and in scenes to come—hints at conquering. Why would they march a deadly army of ghouls on the capital cities if they did not intend to kill a whole bunch of the population, leaving us vulnerable? Why would they want us to be vulnerable if they only wanted to speak and be heard?

I theorize that Wood modeled his screenplay after standard science fiction tropes without thinking them all the way through. I think he liked the idea that the aliens wanted to save Earthlings from themselves rather than conquer, but he couldn't make that cohere with the conflict and peril that the genre demanded at the time. He put in scary monsters and super

---

[60] Despite his wonderfully florid gestures, Bunny's acting in this scene is unfortunate. His line readings are flat and stilted and his eye movements make it look as if he's not paying attention. When thinking of him, I tend to replace his performance in my mind with Bill Murray's delicious portrayal of him in *Ed Wood*.

[61] None of this is in the screenplay. The scene ends with "Report to me when this has been accomplished." I wish I could have looked at the way Wood punctuated these lines.

creeps, but neglected to reconsider them in light of the aliens' central motivation; he put in a peaceful central motivation, and neglected to reconsider it in light of the scary monsters and super creeps. Some of the atmospheric inconsistency of the film (that it feels like a conquer-Earth narrative and isn't one), and many of the specific inconsistencies of the film, result from this baseline incongruity.

Dissolve back to the mother ship. Cut back to Earth. A black police car speeds by on the dirt road, right to left. A saucer floats by in the sky, right to left. A white car zooms by the camera, right to left; a just-readable sign saying SAN FERNANDO is framed center-shot. In a bit of shoe-leather, the police car parks before a black backdrop, and Lt. Harper, Col. Edwards, and Kelton get out. Kelton waits at the car and the other two walk onto the Trents' patio, intercut with a saucer shot for no apparent reason. Finally, three protagonists from separate story threads meet. It is minute 52 of 78.

Col. Edwards begins to ask Jeff and Paula about their "strange experience." Wood does something right here: he elides the conversation. We cut to the same old saucer-landing-in-photo-cemetery shot, and then back to the patio. A pull-back centers Paula, saying "After that, the police brought me home," and revealing three Coke bottles on the table, two mostly empty; Lt. Harper is smoking. These visual details denote that time has passed. The camera move, pulling back, indicates a conclusion,[62] and Paula's words indicate she's finishing up a story. Good job, Eddie.

The Trents describe the phenomena a little more, including seeing a "glowing ball" moving toward the cemetery, in contradiction to the "Well, haven't you heard?" conversation between the policemen, as the man who said that line 14 minutes ago sits and listens.[63]

Cut to the exterior of what is meant to be Eros's ship. Faux-Lugosi

---

[62] Pushing in indicates an opening. A classic example is the "Dignity, always dignity" sequence from *Singin' in the Rain*, when Gene Kelly tells the story of how he got going in Hollywood. The sequence opens by pushing in on Kelly before we dissolve to a series of flashbacks. When these end, we return to the close-up on Kelly, and then we pull back and move on. There are a *lot* of examples exactly like this across classical Hollywood. It's part of the grammar of cinema: push in for opening, pull back for conclusion. Wood either learned this or noticed it, and implemented it here.

[63] As a previous explanation of that scene indicated (p. 64), Harper's earlier scene originally meant that sometimes the saucer glows and sometimes it doesn't. But I'm not giving Wood this one. That scene failed, so it casts doubt on this one.

emerges. Real Lugosi walks through the location cemetery, in his actual last moment in the film.

Back to the patio. The party hears and smells something. Tension builds (sort of). Faux-Lugosi advances on Kelton, first near the car and then onto the patio. Kelton fires his gun to no effect and gets knocked down. Lt. Harper fires his gun, and the other three characters *stand still* while faux-Lugosi gets closer and closer to them, slowly enough to be outrun easily. Cut to the photo-cemetery and a throbbing glow on the horizon. An electric-charge sound occurs and a ray of light spears out from the horizon, and faux-Lugosi drops to the patio floor. Moments later, Col. Edwards lifts his cape away to reveal . . . a skeleton! EEEK!

Col. Edwards and Lt. Harper revive poor Kelton, who is badly spooked. Duke Moore (Harper) decides to act this scene with an amused, indulgent air, which seems a more and more dissonant choice every time I watch it.

Dissolve to a car parking by the cemetery, from which disembark (in no hurry) all five non-dead characters in the previous scene: Paula, Jeff, Kelton, Lt. Harper, and Col. Edwards. Multiple elements of the film (the danger Paula's in, where she runs after she's attacked) depend on the cemetery being in walking distance to the Trents' house, so they shouldn't have had to drive there. I can think of no diegetic reasons for this disparity. A non-diegetic reason involves Paula having a place to wait before she's put in danger, which is a bad reason to make this move, but probably the correct one.

Kelton stays behind at the car (again) with Paula in the back seat,[64] while the other three men walk through the studio cemetery looking for . . . well, even they don't know.

---

[64] She remains behind because this is a movie and she has to be in peril at least once more, but the argument about her remaining behind contains a minor contradiction with a silly bow of sexism on top:

LT. HARPER

Modern women.

COL. EDWARDS

Yeah, they been that way **all down through the ages.**

The script is less contradictory, if no less sexist. Edwards's reply is "From all I've seen, they've been the same for ages," meaning no, it's not about modern women, all women are argumentative and always have been.

JEFF

What do you expect to find out here?

LT. HARPER

Well, there's only one answer to that, Mr. Trent. We'll know when we find it.

Meanwhile, Eros and Tanna prepare to receive visitors. Tor is sent off for Paula and Kelton, while Vampira is tasked with nothing. The three men gathered at Clay's grave (Jeff, Harper, and Edwards) suddenly notice the throbbing glow on the horizon, after not noticing it at all this whole time, and decide to head that way.

Back at the car, Tor takes out Kelton, and then goes for Paula, whose screams evidently do not reach across the cemetery.

The three men trade inept dialogue—

LT. HARPER

Boy, how could anything that big hide for so long a time?

—and Eros instructs Tanna to let them in. Throughout all this, Wood expends screen time on Eros and Tanna walking back and forth across the ship set to alternately activate devices and gaze out the window. It's less than ten seconds per trip, but it's deeply unnecessary for the set to be blocked so as to waste the audience's time like this. It's the very definition of shoe-leather.

Eros and Tanna explain to each other for the audience's benefit that they plan to kill these three Earthlings, and that they feel sad about the waste of it. In the scene before Tor grabs Paula:

EROS

These are the same men who have been so close so often. They must be halted before they can inform others about us.

And now:

EROS

```
Well, wouldn't it be better to kill a few now
than, with their meddling, permit them to
destroy the entire universe?
```

The implication seems to be that because these men have discovered Eros's ship, they must be killed. Previously, Eros and Bunny were both angry that Earth leaders refused to acknowledge them. Why would men who acknowledge the aliens' existence have to die, when acknowledgment is the aliens' goal? How does the meddling of these specific men lead to the destruction of the universe?

This confusion joins with the confusion of whether the aliens are here to conquer, or communicate, or *what,* until the present scene bears an almost pleasant anticipation. We have no idea what will happen when these sets of characters meet, because we can't be at all sure what their motivations are for the meeting. Such uncertainty and unpredictability would be an asset at this point in the movie if it didn't derive from poor storytelling.

In the Earthlings come. They act hostile, trying to take control of the situation with commands and pointing guns, despite being *inside a UFO,* a space of which they have no knowledge, one that is the known territory of another *species.*

The scene that follows is long, tiring, badly written, badly acted, profoundly unscientific, and incredibly funny. Eros gets the lion's share of the dialogue, for better or worse. The scene does communicate an actual idea, if an idiotic one, and Wood gets out of his own way as a director and editor, letting the dialogue pull most of the communicative weight. That means the mechanics of filmmaking in this long scene are not as worthy of analysis as the text. The angles vary between full shots, medium shots, shot/reverse-shots, and closeups of the different characters. The simplicity of this work unfortunately gives Wood's dopey ideas enough rope to hang themselves more effectively than in other, less coherently shot and edited sequences.

Since the dialogue is specifically at issue here, I'm going to annotate it.

```
JEFF
You fiend!

EROS
I? A fiend? I am a soldier of our planet! I? A
fiend?[65] We did not come here as enemies. We
came only with friendly intentions.[66] To talk.
To ask your aid.

COL. EDWARDS
Our aid?

EROS
Yes. Your aid for the whole universe. But your
governments of Earth refused even to accept our
existence. Even though you've seen us, heard
our messages, you still refused to accept us.[67]

COL. EDWARDS
Why is it so important that you want to contact
the governments of our Earth?[68]
```

[65] Dudley Manlove pours it on in performance here, but repetition makes the question seem less profound, not more. Adding another few lines in between might have made the repeated line work better. The incredulousness with which he says it indicates that Eros will explain why the Earthlings are the true fiends. Eventually he almost succeeds at this, but such a rhetorical strategy only works if he repeats the "fiend" theme throughout the speech and follows up on it at the end.

[66] As previously explored, this is difficult to believe.

[67] Refusal of the aliens' existence isn't the whole truth, based on the conversation in Gen. Roberts's office and Col. Edwards's job "in charge of saucer field activity."

[68] GOOD QUESTION, COLONEL. As in the scene between Eros and

EROS

Because of death. Because all you of Earth are idiots![69]

JEFF

Now you just hold on, buster.

EROS

No, you hold on.[70] First was your firecracker, a harmless explosive. Then your hand grenade. They began to kill your own people a few at a time. Then the bomb. Then a larger bomb. Many people are killed at one time.[71] Then your scientists stumbled upon the atom bomb. Split the atom. Then the hydrogen bomb, where you actually explode the air itself.[72] Now you [audio jump][73] brings the total destruction of the entire universe, served by our sun.[74] The

---

Tanna on pp. 51-54, an answer to this question would make a real scene. Maybe Eros has a good answer…

69 …or maybe not. The two sentences in this line are equally funny, but Eros delivers the first sentence like a dramatic eleven-year-old.

70 Eros's rhetoric is not improving.

71 Somehow this portion of the speech feels longer than a semester on the history of munitions. We get it; militaries continue to develop bombs, each larger than the last.

72 I am no scientist, but I'm fairly sure this is not how the H-bomb works.

73 In the script, this is the line (which in the film is nipped in the middle by some kind of audio problem): "Now you can destroy whole cities of people in one big explosion. There is only one step left until you and your Earthman's stupidity brings the total destruction of the entire Universe served by our sun." (punctuation Wood's)

74 "Served by our sun." This line implies that Eros's race comes from a planet in the same solar system as Earth, doesn't it? But that's impossible, isn't it? Also, his recorded message said "from a planet of your galaxy," which is extremely unspecific, but at least more likely than him being from

only explosion left is the Solaronite.

COL. EDWARDS

Why, there's no such thing.

EROS

Perhaps to you. But we've known it for centuries. Your scientists will stumble upon it as they have all the others.[75] But the juvenile minds you possess will not comprehend its strength until it's too late.

COL. EDWARDS

You're way above our heads.[76]

EROS

The Solaronite is a way to explode the actual particles of sunlight.

COL. EDWARDS

Why, that's impossible.[77]

EROS

Even now, your scientists are working on a way

---

a planet "served by our sun," or than the entire universe being "served by our sun."

[75] Vague pronoun usage. Subtract ten points.

[76] I'm interested in this line. It seems like it's trying to placate Eros, to get him to be helpful instead of insulting, but Edwards delivers it with some contempt. It does little except agree with Eros's prior line. I really do not know what it's for, except to provide a beat between Eros delivering an insult and a piece of information.

[77] Look at Edwards's last three lines. Two lines beginning with "Why," and ending with contradictions of what's just been said, and one that's needless assent. Bad, bad writing.

to harness the sun's rays. The rays of sunlight are minute particles.[78] Is it so far from your imagination they cannot do as I have suggested?[79]

COL. EDWARDS

Why, a particle of sunlight can't even be seen or measured.[80]

EROS

Can you see or measure an atom?[81] Yet you can explode one. A ray of sunlight is made up of many atoms.[82]

JEFF

So what if we do develop this Solaronite bomb? We'd be even a stronger nation than now.[83]

EROS

Stronger. You see? You see? Your stupid minds! Stupid! Stupid![84]

---

[78] Technically I think this is true, light being both a particle and a wave, but I can't believe Wood knew the science behind it at the time.

[79] This sentence makes no grammatical sense. "They" has an unclear antecedent. Subtract 20 points.

[80] "Why," again.

[81] Actually, yes, we can measure atoms.

[82] No, it's made up of *particles*. Focus, Eros!

[83] It's not important in context of this movie's scads of errors, but this line vocalizes the assumption that Eros is talking just to Americans, not the whole world.

[84] I have seen many an audience laugh at this line, this famed, oft-quoted, oft-used-to-sum-up-the-stupidity-of-*Plan-9* line. I don't know how Wood could have written it seriously, nor how Dudley Manlove could have delivered it without knowing how ridiculous it sounded. I see his point, that all Earth men think about is exploding things and having military power, but throwing a tantrum is not going to get his point across.

JEFF

That's all I'm taking from you!
[JEFF LEAPS AT EROS]

LT. HARPER

Get back here, you jerk! Let him finish.[85]

EROS

It's because of men like you that all must be destroyed. Headstrong, violent! No use of the mind God gave you.[86]

JEFF

You talk of God?

EROS

You also think it impossible that we, too, might think of God?[87] [TO COL. EDWARDS] You, who wear the uniform of your country. You see, I wear the uniform of my country.[88] Yes, we've had to use drastic means to get to you, but

---

[85] It's true that Eros has not finished his lecture on Solaronite, but "let him finish," is a weird sentiment for Lt. Harper of all people to offer up. It would have been a better line for Edwards, and different phrasing would have been better still. In the script, I found that Wood agreed with me, in part:

HARPER

Get back here, you fool.

COLONEL

Calm down, Jeff. Let him finish.

[86] The sincerity with which this line is delivered cracks me up every time.

[87] The awkwardness with which this line was written cracks me up every time. Still, it's a crime against every writer's ear. Subtract 30 points and see me after class.

[88] At the beginning of the scene he said he was "a soldier of our *planet*."

you left us no alternative.[89] When you have the Solaronite, you have nothing. Nor does the universe.[90]

COL. EDWARDS

You speak of Solaronite, but just what is it?

EROS

Take a can of your gasoline. Say this can of gasoline is the sun. Now you spread a thin line of it to a ball, representing the Earth. Now, the gasoline represents the sunlight, the sun particles. Here we saturate the ball with the gasoline, the sunlight. Then we put a flame to the ball. The flame will speedily travel around the Earth, back along the line of gasoline to the can, or the sun itself. It will explode this source, and spread to every place that gasoline, our sunlight, touches.[91] Explode the sunlight here, gentlemen, and you explode the universe. Explode the sunlight here, and a chain reaction will occur, direct to the sun itself. And to all the planets that sunlight touches. To every planet in the

---

[89] But Earthlings haven't even developed the weapon yet. Surely there are *many* alternatives to *Plan 9*.

[90] I can't quite parse the antecedent for "nor." The universe has nothing if the human race has nothing and if they do have Solaronite? I think he means to say the universe is screwed if humans develop Solaronite, but the point is badly lost in the sentences.

[91] I should not need to say it, but this is inane. The metaphor doesn't work, but even if it did, the science is daffy.

universe.[92] This is why you must be stopped. This is why any means must be used to stop you. In a friendly manner, or as it seems, you want it.[93]

LT. HARPER

He's mad.[94]

TANNA

Mad? Is it mad that you destroy other people to save yourselves? You have done this. Is it mad that one country must destroy another to save themselves? You have also done this.[95] How then is it mad that one planet must destroy another that threatens the very existence—[96]

---

[92] Whatever Wood's idea is of how light travels through the galaxy, and how close planets are to each other, it is mistaken.

[93] There's no evidence in the movie that the aliens have tried "a friendly manner."

[94] I don't really understand why this is anyone's reaction at this moment in the scene. Maybe the idea is just to discredit Eros? Because what he's saying is too complicated and negative for Lt. Harper to understand, so he's going to write him off as crazy? He could have said "Your science is bad," or "We haven't developed a weapon like that," or "Let's go talk to someone higher up in the government about this to determine if your concerns are valid about the threat we present," or "What's the deal with the ghouls, then?" or even "Shut up." But instead, "He's mad." When I think about it, the likeliest reason for this line is to set up Tanna's little speech, coming next. This is the very laziest kind of writing that exists, when characters say things purely so you can get other characters to say other things.

[95] Something about the rhythm of these lines feels like Wood's trying to be…grand? Biblical? I'm not really sure. The actress doesn't do a bad job, but the lines feel so strange.

EROS

```
[interrupting, pushing Tanna] That's enough!
In my land, women are for advancing the race,
not for fighting man's battles.[97] Life is not
so expensive on my planet. We don't cling to
it like you do. Our entire aim is for the
development of our planet.[98]
```

Phew. That's about seven minutes of scene. The first cut outside the spaceship is to a police car driving along the same dirt road as ever before, and then to Kelton regaining consciousness in the front seat of the police car in the studio. Slow as molasses, a second police car pulls up beside, and Larry questions a distraught Kelton about why he called for backup. It's not a useful scene. Even Vampira walks away from it.

Tor carries Paula . . . somewhere. Cut to Eros gazing out of the daytime window, doomsaying in a dreary voice. He offers the impression that he's been speaking for many hours. In a comedy, we'd cut from him to the other four sprawled in office chairs, snoring.

---

[96] Here she says destroying Earth *is* on the table after all. But it's the only line in the film that says so directly.

[97] [eye-roll]. Also, how can Tanna be an astronaut at all if this is the case?

[98] I truly cannot make sense of these lines. How can you aim to develop a planet without people? What does clinging to life have to do with *anything* that's been said in this scene so far, much less the silly sexism in the prior line? I grasp for meaning, and can only guess that the connection is about humans having to die so that we don't develop Solaronite. Our deaths would sadden us, but not the aliens, because they place little value on individual human (or alien) life. But I'm fumbling around in the dark. The expensiveness of life on Eros's planet seems irrelevant.[c]

[c] Dudley Manlove clearly says "expansive" in the film. The script says "expensive." "Expansive" makes less sense, but "expensive" doesn't make a whole lot more.

At this point, two scenes (really two and a half) are going on simultaneously. The three men and two aliens talk in circles in the spaceship. Outside, in the cemetery, Tor has Paula, while Kelton and Larry search for Paula and the three men. The next few minutes cross-cut these scenes with each other, with fair success. The humans in the ship and the policemen outside it become aware of Tor and Paula at almost the same time. The editing implies that the cops have seen the glow from the ship, too, although the dialogue doesn't. They disarm Tor with a blow to the head, which of course makes no sense, and ADR gives Paula dialogue that also makes no sense, while her mouth does not move.

Back inside the ship, the humans illogically gain the upper hand, and a physical fight of middling quality breaks out. Eros attempts to hurl sciencey stuff at Jeff, while Tanna frantically tries to make the ship take off. Col. Edwards and Lt. Harper get the door open in their own sweet time.

COL. EDWARDS

`Get out of here, Jeff! The ship's on fire!`

How he knows this, I can't say. No fire is visible before he says the line.

The humans flee. Jeff looks back at the destruction he's wrought: a mostly empty room with some toppled equipment and a prone Eros. It is not as disastrous-looking as the music seems to believe it is.

Tanna tries to improve the situation inside the ship, but she is a woman and thus she is panicky and useless. The cast of living humans stands in a line looking up: Col. Edwards, hands comfortably in pockets; Lt. Harper, ever holding his gun; Paula and Jeff, no particular looks on their faces; and Larry, looking approximately like nothing is happening. Kelton stands mostly out of frame. A saucer, afire, lifts out of the photo cemetery. It floats over a spray of city lights. The humans trade some dialogue and reveal the skeleton of Tor.

PAULA

`Have they caught that woman, that thing, yet?`

LT. HARPER

Hey, that's right. There's another ghoul running loose.

COL. EDWARDS

And it's my guess that she'll look like him. With the ship and the ray gun gone, they have no control.

It's unclear whether Paula ever saw Vampira at all. It seemed to be mostly faux-Lugosi pursuing her in the earlier peril sequence. The editing in that sequence somewhat indicates that Vampira sees Paula, but nothing indicates that Paula sees Vampira. Later, she sees Tor, and the other characters definitely do see both Tor and faux-Lugosi, but there's no direct evidence that any of the surviving human characters see Vampira at all.[99]

How do they know there's another ghoul? How does Paula know it's a woman? Further, how do the characters know these are the only three, and that Eros is responsible for all of them?

The film did clarify that Eros was responsible for the ghouls, but it didn't specify the bit about the ray gun. For all Col. Edwards knows, the ghouls could continue to go about their mission indefinitely. Tor could have been skeletonized on purpose, rather than because the ship is leaving and also on fire. *We* know, but that doesn't mean *Edwards* knows. It's a stretch for him to speculate that Vampira will be neutralized too, because the characters have never known (on camera, as part of a scene) what created the ghouls or what caused them to turn into skeletons.

Col. Edwards's entire line here is written as wrap-up, though. Wood needed to tie off the Vampira situation, so he did it without visuals and with this one hasty line, rather than with a more gradual series of lines and information fed to the audience with care.

---

[99] Editing hints that Farmer does, but it's not especially direct. The cops talking about Paula and Farmer's report mention them seeing spirits, plural, but that could be Tor and faux-Lugosi. I'm not trying to be difficult here; I'm trying to say that the character knowledge expressed by these lines has minimal foundation in the film. It's a long-division problem, who knows what and how they know it, and Wood hasn't shown his work.

COL. EDWARDS

We've got to hand it to them, though...they're far ahead of us.

This is a Captain Obvious line, and it portrays Col. Edwards as a big man who can admit when he's outclassed. Yet we could read the line as troubling. The aliens mean harm (probably?), and they have the advantage over us. If they choose to come back—perhaps with Plan 10—we're done for.

Tanna screams into a frame almost entirely filled with smoke, and the saucer explodes. Immediately we cut to Criswell, for the last word.

CRISWELL

My friend, you have seen this incident based on sworn testimony. Can you prove that it didn't happen?

No one can prove a negative. But I'm pretty sure this didn't happen.

CRISWELL

Perhaps on your way home, you will pass someone in the dark, and you will never know it, for they will be from outer space.

I won't know I've passed someone *because* they were from outer space?

CRISWELL

Many scientists believe that another world is watching us this moment. We once laughed at the horseless carriage, the aeroplane, the telephone, the electric light, vitamins, radio, and even television. And now some of us laugh at outer space.

Does anyone laugh at the very *concept* of outer space? (Or at vitamins?[100])

[100] One final theft from the RiffTrax for *Plan 9*.

```
                    CRISWELL
        God help us...in the future.
```

The point of this speech remains unclear to me. When I search through the individual sentences for individual or overall meaning, I can't find any. The very idea of meaning slips through my fingers. Now that you've read almost all of this monograph, I invite you to break down the speech and try to make sense of it yourself, just as I've broken down as much of the rest of the film as I could. If you find any meaning, please let me know.

I do get hung up repeatedly on the last line, and what it's meant to communicate. It's unexpectedly dire. Plenty of B movies end with semi-concealed messages about the terrors of nuclear war and how dangerous it is to play with space-travel technology, but Criswell's words offer a kind of overarching, unspecific pessimism. Are we doomed? Have we been entertained? Perhaps we are not meant to know.

PLAN 9
FROM
OUTER
SPACE
with
BELA LUGOSI
VAMPIRA
LYLE TALBOT
A J. Edward Reynolds Production
Produced and Directed by
Edward D. Wood, Jr.
a DCA release
1
58-294

III: IN SUM

WHAT YOU'VE JUST READ I WROTE BACKWARDS. I DRAFTED THE whole thing, and then, in preparing to write this conclusion, I created an outline of my main ideas and listed the examples I chose to prove them. This outline showed me that I had five things to say about bad movies, and I used *Plan 9 from Outer Space* to say them in great detail.

(1) Bad movies are unconvincing as movies.
(2) They are, instead, successful records of attempts at making movies. This quality means they give the audience a dual, holographic view: of the successful record and of the failed attempt.
(3) Knowing more about the context of a bad movie is crucial to understanding and analyzing it, but is hardly a license to excuse it.
(4) Bad movies are teaching tools for making and studying good movies.
(5) As such, they are best studied in aggregate.

A sub-point, better made about other films than *Plan 9*, is that bad movies are wonderfully surprising, because they upend audience expectations. *Plan 9* does this somewhat, but other bad movies do it better.

(1)

Many examples exist of why *Plan 9 from Outer Space* is unconvincing as a movie. It's extremely inconsistent, on a scene level. Its special effects are terrible. It includes scenes that try to clear up problems the audience hasn't even thought of—the conversation about why Vampira was buried in the ground and Lugosi was buried in a crypt, for instance, or Lt. Harper's poorly written attempt to explain why the flying saucer that lands in the cemetery sometimes has a glow and sometimes doesn't. The nine non-intersecting aspects of the movie's plot. The time frame of the funerals and the discovery of the gravediggers' bodies. So many elements in this movie push the audience out of the filmgoing experience and make her realize she is watching a simulation, rather than pulling her *into* the simulation, letting her forget the metatextual aspects of her experience.

Of course, we never fully believe we are *part of* a movie, unless we are children or fools. We are bespelled by what we see on the screen in a particular way, and it's a kind of magic to which we consent. But the spell must be strong enough to put us under. Bad movies have no magic of this kind. Because they can't hypnotize the audience, the audience notices the motion of the hypnotizing agent: the pendulum, the 24 frames per second.

(2)

Plan 9's holographic qualities are especially potent. The wobbling tombstones show us that they are props on a set. The existence of props on a set shows the audience that a movie is being made. The movie being made is on the screen, but it is unconvincing as a movie. So we see both: the wobbling prop and the reality of its existence as a prop, *as well as* the whole cinematic context that tries to seal the illusion of this undertaking as a movie.

The police come to the cemetery immediately after Paula and Farmer drive away from it, which casts doubt on the continuity of the story, which makes us recognize it as a story. Some of us might even see the hand of the creator. We might realize that Wood needed the police to come back to the cemetery somehow, so he just had them drive back, and saw no need to build the bridge between the Paula/Farmer incident and the police returning.

When we feel confused and our train of thought is interrupted by the Hollywood montage, we realize that the movie isn't making sense to us, thus realizing that it is a movie, and that a writer and director and editor (all the same man in this case) forced it to try and make sense.

A filmmaker must understand with complete acuity what the audience knows and what the characters know, and how these banks of knowledge differ from each other. If we realize Paula is aware of Vampira, when we have no positive proof that she has *seen* Vampira, the scrim between us and her collapses. We become aware that the same person created everything we're seeing—characters, conflicts, secrets, lies.

Toward the end, when five of the main characters pile into a car and drive to a cemetery that's in walking distance, we realize that either Wood has lost track of his geography, or he needed the car to come to the cemetery for some reason not explained by the plot. The plot is one side of the holograph (the spell, the illusion) and the reason is the other side (the set, the props). We see him trying to make the movie, and we see the movie he's trying to make, both at the same time. The illusion is too thin to disguise the creator; in this case, the Wizard's light and sound show does not distract anyone in Dorothy's party.

(3)

Back there somewhere I wrote about the stock footage/running time context of *Plan 9*, and how it explains but does not excuse the resulting bad sequences. External factors like the cost of film and equipment, which were astronomical in 1956 compared to the cost of a decent HD camcorder today, also matter. The way *Plan 9* mixes up peaceful aliens with hostile intent, and winds up with a confusing semi-enemy, is part of the film's context, as the film was trying to adhere to two separate and conflicting trends. Some of the stiffness of its acting and the poor quality of its special effects can be explained (not excused) with context, too, though not all.[101]

One element of *Plan 9*'s context I didn't really write about is how its genre impacts its quality. Others have written generously about *Plan 9*'s multifarious genre, its mishmash of science fiction, horror, zombie movie, and military film. I'd like to revise that to say it includes *aspects* of all those genres, but it does not succeed at fully embracing or embodying any of them. At the time it was released, significantly, genre films were almost never of high quality. Pre-*2001: A Space Odyssey*, science fiction, fantasy, and horror were not taken especially seriously by filmmakers, critics, or audiences. A handful of good genre films came out in the late 1950s: *The Incredible Shrinking Man* (1957), *The Fly* (1958). But mostly, a list of sci-fi movies from the era reads like a catalogue of *MST3K* movies. *Plan 9* is an unusually bad film in a mostly bad genre, and this context matters when assessing it.

Additional contextual elements are the temporary popularity of some of the cast and the lasting popularity of Lugosi's Dracula character. Vampira and Lugosi are (probably) dressed to make the audience remember how much they liked these characters on other screens, and hopefully to endear them to the entertainment on *this* screen. Criswell is totally forgotten today, but he was a fixture on local TV at the time, which made his appearances and voiceover valuable to 1959 audiences. These choices seem strange to a 21st century audience lacking context—who is that lady and why does she look like that? who is that guy and why does he talk like that?—but made sense then.

Ultimately, there's no way to forgive *Plan 9* its flaws just because it was made in a certain way at a certain time. But we can understand and assess it with a more sophisticated eye and mind if we consider that way and time than we can if we look on it as a free-floating page torn away from a book of film history.

[101] As a parallel example, the laughable quality of some computer-generated effects in the mid-1990s can be explained with context—limitations in software and memory, the available skill and experience of effects makers. But Pixar was already doing business by then, so...some, but not all.

(4)

Students of cinema can learn volumes of lessons from this one film:

- Editing cannot carry the full weight of blocking a sequence of scenes.
- The main plot of a movie must be front and center. The scenes and sequences in a movie must have some proportionate relationship to the importance of the plot element communicated in the scene.
- Base-level continuity (not, like, how the glasses are arranged on the café table or how many buttons are on someone's coat) depends on three Ls: lighting, location, and landmarks. Without carrying these elements over between edits, the audience will not assume your characters are in the same time, place, or situation.
- Don't waste the audience's time on shoe-leather. Nor on dialogue that waffles, unless you're carefully building character over a long period of time.
- If you're filming a sequence mainly of dialogue, make damn sure that dialogue is interesting and not stupid.
- Montages should call back to what has already occurred in the film and hint at what comes next. They should not introduce important characters.
- Show stakes, don't just tell them. Remember, this is a *motion picture*.[102] The best way to explain danger is to *show* the outcome of that danger when not avoided.

(5)

There is so much more to learn from bad movies. *Plan 9 from Outer Space* doesn't make all possible film mistakes, although it surely makes a lot of them. The only way to understand the thousands of small and large ways a movie can go sideways is to watch a ton of them and take notes.

[102] Stolen from *MST3K: The Dead Talk Back*.

For example, Criswell's voiceover, though unhelpful, rarely duplicates the action on the screen in a way that renders the voiceover superfluous.[103] The scene on p. 68 does this, as the visuals already did the work that Criswell does a second time, but it's just about the only occasion. Even if a film uses voiceover to make sense of what's on screen rather than overexplaining it, screenwriting teachers discourage the technique, as it can lead to lazy writing. (Why would you take the trouble to show something when you can narrate it instead?) Wood uses voiceover to bridge gaps in his incompetence, not in his laziness, but many filmmakers do the opposite. Further, there's always the negative example of a film like *Monster a Go-Go* (1965), in which filming produced very little usable sound, so the movie relies on voiceover instead of dialogue. That's incompetence, too, but of a different kind than Wood's.

Figuring out what's going wrong in a movie becomes a worthy puzzle. Some movies take themselves much too seriously. Others cast actors who have no chemistry with each other or the camera. Still others depend on titillation or gimmicks, either of which can fall flat or offend. Pacing problems can sink a movie; too much money can make a movie tedious; a script that changes too often or remains too rigid can overturn everything good about a movie. Combining a lack of budget with an egomaniac at the helm often results in terrible cinema (Wood, Wiseau), but sometimes that combination can create something incredible (Kenneth Anger, Darren Aronofsky).

Patterns, not individual elements, characterize and predict bad movies. A few of the problems in *Plan 9* are part of these patterns: the poor usage of day for night, cutaways disguising mistakes or bad takes, filler and shoe-leather scenes, the triangulation of genre with time period. These characteristics exist across a huge swath of bad movies. Yet for the most part, *Plan 9* is lit well (if sometimes a bit strongly), and its music is not overtly terrible. Wood knows how to use an establishing shot to show the audience where we're going, and knows not to linger too long on it. His scenes, despite how badly their dialogue is written, all have beginnings,

---

[103] The cut of *Blade Runner* (1982) with voiceover is a terrific example of this error. The voiceover doesn't explore the inside of Deckard's head or any of the film's abundant subtext, it just reexplains what's already on screen.

middles, and ends. Because *Plan 9* is certainly terrible, it's hard to remember to give credit to stuff like this.

But plenty of movies have problems *Plan 9* doesn't. Bad lighting and bad music are endemic to sub-par movies. Inexperienced filmmakers often allow establishing shots to hang out onscreen for the better part of a minute, whether to hammer home the point to the audience or to let a music cue finish or because they don't have a good grasp of pacing.[104] And poor writers will chop off scenes in the middle rather than truly concluding them, or will fail to give the scene a middle at all, often robbing it of a purpose.

The best way to understand what a bad filmmaker like Wood is doing wrong, and what he's doing right, is to watch so many movies of all qualities that the patterns jump out. You begin to notice what all the bad movies have in common just as easily as you notice what all the good ones do. The more you watch, the starker these contrasts become, and the more the established grammar of cinema makes sense. In the right hands, violating that grammar has remarkable results (early Brian De Palma), but in the wrong hands, it just makes a mess (James Nguyen).

(SUB-POINT)

If you can't believe me about bad film as a teaching tool, consider it as a change of pace from the irritating rigor of mainstream American film. Most of what goes on the big screen in the current moment in the US is proscribed, and prescribed, down to the minute. There are three carefully proportioned acts with predictable plot moves and character choices, dependent in their particulars on genre. There's bloat in the third act, usually, although sometimes toward the end of the second. The color palette is showy and artificial. Shakycam abounds, especially in difficult emotional scenes or action scenes for which the actors are inadequately prepared. Most of the film is staged to be watchable on a small screen,

[104] A movie from 2013 that will drive you to the nuthouse, *A Talking Cat!?!*, favors establishing shots over substantive shots. They often have no relationship to the plot, nor do they even establish where the next scene will take place, sometimes (which is the whole point of an *establishing* shot), and they last for ages.

which means a preference for medium shots and close-ups rather than wide and landscape shots. Plots revolve around miscommunications or grudges or central personality flaws. The women are thin and the men are ideally tousled.

I am so weary of these characteristics that I barely follow contemporary cinema anymore. Friends tell me this or that movie is super good and really different, so I watch, and no, it isn't. Around one film I watch per year genuinely is different, but it's never the one I think it will be, and it's *definitely* never one the Oscars have lauded.

This supreme boredom—and I know it's not attractive—leads me to weird rabbit-holes. It leads me almost anywhere that can offer me a surprise. Most reliably, it leads me to bad movies. I find absolute delight in a movie that breaks all the rules, even if that movie does not hold together and I could never sanely recommend it. I don't watch these movies out of masochism or misanthropy. I watch them because they do what their higher-quality cousins cannot: they show me something I have never seen before.

All the ways in which *Plan 9 from Outer Space* should make sense and doesn't, should be decent and isn't—those missing qualities, if fulfilled, would make it just like every other movie. As a passable movie, it would sit among dozens of similar B pictures from the late 1950s, in reasonably good company on a forgotten library shelf. As a bad movie, it is unique, shining all alone in the darkest cavern of bad art.

ADIEU

I hope you have found this useful. I hope you watch some bad movies with a spirit of exploration, with a notepad, with a ready laugh. I hope you can read *Plan 9 from Outer Space* as a failure that has a great deal to teach, or as a success in chronicling sheer will and ambition. I hope you write or make something better, but I hope you see that writing and making as an act of building on the bad as well as the good. No discourse, no art form, is complete without both.

BIBLIOGRAPHY

BOOKS

Craig, Rob. *Ed Wood, Mad Genius: A Critical Study of the Films*. Jefferson, NC: McFarland & Company Publishers, 2009.

Grey, Rudolph. *Nightmare of Ecstasy: The Life and Art of Edward D. Wood, Jr.* Los Angeles: Feral House, 1992.

Mason, Tom, ed. *Plan 9 from Outer Space: The Original Uncensored and Uncut Screenplay by Edward D. Wood, Jr.* Newbury Park, CA: Malibu Graphics, Inc., 1990.

Rausch, Andrew J. and Charles E. Pratt, Jr. *The Cinematic Misadventures of Ed Wood*. Albany, GA: BearManor Media, 2015.

Wood, Edward D., Jr. *Hollywood Rat Race*. New York: Four Walls Eight Windows, 1998.

FILMS

Best Worst Movie. Directed by Michael Paul Stevenson. OJO Entertainment, 2009.

Ed Wood. Directed by Tim Burton. Touchstone Pictures, 1994.

Ed Wood: Look Back in Angora. Directed by Ted Newsom. Rhino Home Video, 1994.

Flying Saucers Over Hollywood: The Plan 9 Companion. Directed by Mark Patrick Carducci. Atomic Pictures, 1992.

Plan 9 from Outer Space. Directed by Edward D. Wood, Jr. Reynolds Pictures, 1957.

ACKNOWLEDGMENTS

My love and gratitude to:

Neil Snowdon.

Everyone at PS.

The entire galaxy of MiSTies and Traxians—the fandom and the creators.

Andrew J. Rausch, Bill Corbett, Dana Gould—wonderfully generous men.. Christopher Higgs.

My father, whose snicker I miss terribly.

Matt above all—again.